Star Struck

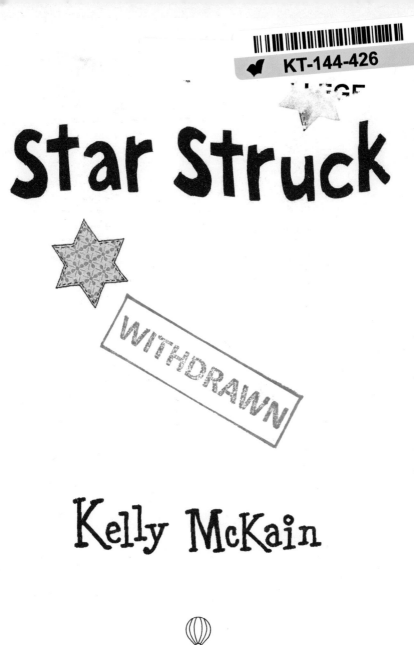

WITHDRAWN

Kelly McKain

USBORNE

4.12.13

LUCY ♥ DANIEL 4 EVER

BFF

My
totally secret
journal

by ~~WITHDRAWN~~

Lucy Jessica Hartley

⭐ L + ⭐ J + ⭐ J

POP

Thursday the 7th of April

at 10.17 o'clock exactly.
Waiting by the phone for
this really exciting thing.

Hi! Lucy Jessica Hartley here! This thing is
soooooo exciting I'm even starting a new journal
to tell you about it. Of course it might all still
end up in tears if I don't get in, and then this
journal will have about half a page of writing in
because my life will go back to its usual state
of boringness!

Hang on, you're probably not getting what
I'm on about. Mum says I have this habit of
starting at the end and ending up back at the
middle. Sometimes when I'm trying to explain
about something, she goes, "Deep breath, Lucy,
and start at the beginning." So I will.

Huuuuuuuuuuuuuuurrrr!

↖ Me having a
deep breath

5

So here I am, *at the beginning* of something *mega-ly* exciting (I hope!).

What happened is that about one week ago I was hanging out with my **BFF** (**BFF** means Best Friends Forever, **BTW**) (**BTW** means By The Way, **BTW**) the fabulicious Julietta Garcia Perez Benedicionatorio – Jules – and the toptastic Matilda-Jane Van der Zwan – Tilda.

We were walking through the market getting some hot dogs and looking at embroidery thread for making friendship bracelets. We are mad on them at the moment and we make them all the time. In fact, you can pin them to your skirt and then carry on making them secretly in class while listening to the teacher, although when I pointed out to Mr. Wright in English that we were still *fully engaged* (as he puts it) with the lesson, he didn't quite agree, and we had to sit with our hands on our desks for the whole time.

Anyway, I've got off the point (which is something else I do a lot, according to Mum). So what happened was, we were walking round the market, with Jules cheerful because the hot-dog man hadn't put onions on hers without asking and Tilda cheerful because her dad had said she could have one Diet Coke while we were out. Normally she's allowed no fizzy drinks whatsoever because they make her go hyper and – (*Whoops,* I've gone off the point again, but read *Makeover*

7

Magic, my first journal, if you want to know the *sizzling* secret details!)

So we were all happy, which can sometimes not happen as Jules gets a bit moody with Tilda about us being a three now. It used to be only me and Jules on our own in BFFness, right up to 4 months ago when Tilda came to Tambridge High and –

Eeeeeek!!! I can't believe I have gone off the actual point *again*! It must be that all the excitement is making my brain spin.

Okay, so we sat down on a bench, and there was a local newspaper someone had left.

I was flicking through it to get to the horoscopes and I suddenly saw this advert

Extras Wanted!

Local people of all ages required to work as background artistes in major new British period drama,

Passionate Indiscretions.

To apply, please send your name, address, contact number, age, height and measurements to:

Cherry Pip Productions,
12 Burlington Court, London

We will contact suitable applicants by phone on the 7th of April. If you apply, please ensure that you are available on the 8th of April for auditions and from the 11th to the 17th of April for filming.

PROFESSIONAL ATTITUDE ESSENTIAL.

Well, I read it out and we all got madly excited because they are making an actual **MOVIE** in our actual **TOWN**!!! At first I was thinking that background artistes are people who paint the fake scenery for outside windows on film sets, but brainy Tilda explained that it's really the same as *extras*, the people who are in the background of the actual film!!! Of course we all three instantly wanted to be in it!!! For a minute we were *devastated* because it was in the week and then we realized that it was actually the Easter holidays, so we thought *Yay*!

Then me and Jules were busy laughing about how we might be in a *period* drama, i.e. a drama about a Q! Q is our secret code word for *period*, so we can talk about it at school when boys are there ('cos P is too obvious). But then brainy Tilda also explained that *period drama* means an old-fashioned film where the women all have Heaving Bosoms and the men all do reckless horse-riding up lanes and swim in lakes in their breeches and that. So it's nothing to do with *starting* after all.

We tore out the ad, and we all went back to my house to write our applications together professionally as a three. In Jules's house it is impossible to write things professionally. This is 'cos of all the *kerfuffle* (cool word) of her mum and dad practising their salsa dancing to loud music in the living room while going "*Yeeoww!*", and of JJ playing rock, and of Benito and Benita running around with their talking Luke Skywalkers and of Hombrito just barking. (Hombrito is their dog, **BTW**, in case you were thinking "*Eh?*")

Plus, we haven't even *been* round Tilda's yet 'cos it's just her and her dad at home (her mum died when she was little, but she doesn't really talk about it). Apparently Tilda's dad is usually working in his study, so she says she likes to come to somewhere where there is *something Happening*. From my point of perspective it's better round mine or Jules's 'cos Tilda's dad is totally stricty about food, and the only munchies available would be the sort of things Tilda gets in her lunchbox like sunflower-seed bars and fruit in its *Natural State* instead of made into *Winders* or *Frubes* or whatever.

Anyway, when we'd written out our applications, we walked down to the post box linking arms all the way for luck and ceremoniously sent them off, by hooking our little fingers together and shaking our hands up and down 3 times.

So today I am on *tenterhooks* (whatever *they* are?! – maybe hooks for holding up tents??) because it is the day of deciding who will get an audition to be an extra in *Passionate Indiscretions*, and we have all been waiting nervously by our phones since about, like, 6.42 a.m. Plus, we've got our mobiles ready, so we can let each other know *immediately* if anything happens without blocking up the other person's phone line. Ingenious or what? I should get extra science points off Mrs. Stepton for my logical thinking on this issue, because now I am her favourite it is expected of me to be a *shining Example*.

Eeeeeeeeeeekkkkkkkk! The mobile's ringing! It's Tilda! Hang on...

She got an audition!!!!!

Yesssssss!!!!!!!!!

That's so brill!!!!!!!!!

Erm… Why isn't *my* phone ringing?

Mum has just tried to come in here and ring Nan (Delia) for a chat.

Nan likes to be called Delia 'cos she reckons being a nan makes her feel old, so if I say Delia that's who I'm talking about!

I explained about the mobile and house phone system and how I'm waiting for a *vital* call about the audition and could she please just this once go down the road and use the payphone on the corner?

She went, "Oh, marvellous! I mean, I pay the bills, I bought you a mobile, which I also pay for, and now I've got to go down the road to make a call! Do you want anything from the shop as well, while I'm out?"

It's nice to have such an understanding mother at this sort of nerve-making time. I asked for a Twix and 'cos I'm a Model Daughter I did even offer her 50p to put in the payphone, but she just wandered off muttering. I know how she feels. Call boxes are really pricey these days and 50p doesn't get you very far. Probably only to Bournemouth or something.

At least Mum coming in here took my mind off the fact that the house phone is STILL NOT RINGING! Now I am totally back on to thinking about it.

In my application to be in the film I really showed my *Professional Attitude*. Like, I even did it on my swirly pattern notepaper, which is my best kind that I only use for very important business. They *have* to ring me for an audition, don't they? Especially when they have rung Tilda. They must *know* that BFF have to do this kind of important stuff together as a three.

Hang on, I will stick the photocopy of my application in here. Mum said having a *Professional Attitude* means making photocopies of stuff *for your records* so we all did, even though it was 10p a sheet in the Spend and Save. That was okay for Jules and Tilda but I ended up writing quite a lot. Anyway, I will put it in here to see what you think.

Name: Lucy Jessica Hartley

Address: 4 The Meadows, Barnaby Road, Sherborne, Dorset.

Height: 1m 50cm. But that is not a fixed thing. What I mean is, I am really good at walking in VERY high heels because of the practice I had going down the runway at London Fashion Week (runway is American for catwalk, BTW). I was on the runway because I had won the Hey Girls! magazine Fantasy Fashion Competition and I was modelling my creation (my life's ambition is to be an Actual Real Fashion Designer, BTW).

Anyway, I promise I would not let the high heels show under my hoopy skirt-thing. But on the other hand, if you think I am too tall I can sort of stoop down or even walk on my

knees so long as you
can provide those padded things
like cyclists wear so I don't get a
problem with my cruciate ligament. I
know this is a hazard of too much
kneeling because Dad got one by fixing the
plumbing under the sink. (Mum said it was
more like a case of skivalitis, but she's not
medically trained either, so I don't know
who was right.)

Of course, that was while Dad was still living
here and before he decided to CRUELLY
ABANDON us to move in with Uncle Ken in the
town centre. I still don't fully get why he left,
but it is something to do with wanting to be a
rock and roll star and also 16 again. I pointed
out to Mum that without a time machine that
is impossible, and also it means I wouldn't even
exist, so it would be a bit rubbish for me.

But according to her, Dad leaving is called a midlife crisis and is quite usual in men who <u>never properly grew up in the first place</u>.

  Anyway, when Dad first moved out it turned <u>my</u> life upside-down and I was in <u>tumultuous turmoil</u> wondering why he would choose a manky curry-and-feet-smelling flat with a toilet that has <u>never set eyes on a loo brush</u> (also according to Mum) instead of us. But now it's mainly okay and Mum and Dad can talk to each other nicely (well, most of the time), and me and Alex (my little bro, BTW) are slowly adjusting, like Mum told her friend Gloria on the phone the other day. I'm just telling you about this parent stuff to let you know that I have been through a Difficult Time but that it is mainly sorted out now, and it will not affect my Professional Attitude.

Measurements:

Erm, not sure what you mean
about this. I normally take an age
10 to 12 even though I am a very-
nearly-teenager, because I have a svelte
figure like a model (as my BFF Tilda calls
it). My other BFF Jules just now said she
reckons we should measure ourselves
round the erm, well, the you-know-whats,
and the waist and hips. I am a 30-20-30
(apparently you measure it in inches, like
pizzas). Well, hopefully I will be in a couple of
weeks. Just between us, at the moment I
wish my you-know-whats would grow a bit
more, as I am right now in the smallest bra
size it is possible to actually <u>get</u>.

BTW, my BFF Tilda mentioned that all the
actresses in <u>period dramas</u> have Heaving
Bosoms. I have to be honest and say I don't

think I could get mine to <u>heave</u> exactly,
but in an emergency I would obviously do
my best.

Okay, well, I have to go now 'cos Jules
and Tilda finished their applications ages
ago and they are getting bored waiting for
me. So just to add –

pick me,

pleeeeeeeeeeeeeeeaaaaaaaaaaaaaa
aaaaaaaaaaaaaaaassssssssssssssssssssss
ssssssssssssssssssseeeeeeeeeee!!!!!!!!!!!!!

Love,

Lucy Jessica Hartley

xxxxxx

PS Please also pick Tilda Van der
Zwan and Julietta Garcia Perez
Benedicionatorio. Thanks!

Yessity, yes, yes! The phone just rang this second. It was this lady called Ramona Blunt who has a bossy voice like a dog trainer. Before I could even say *"Hartley residence, to whom do I have the pleasure of speaking?"* in my posh telephone voice, Ramona Blunt had barked at me that Lucy Jessica Hartley has an audition tomorrow at 10 a.m. at the town hall and no latecomers will be admitted. I was just about to say that I in actual fact **AM** Lucy Jessica Hartley when she put the phone down. I dropped the receiver, so it dangled on the wire, while I jumped up and down going *"Yessity-yes-yes!!!"*

Oh wow, I can't believe I might be in an actual FILM!!!!

Then my mobile rang and guess what?

JULES GOT A BARKY PHONE CALL TOO!!!!!!!!!

So we have all three got an audition at 10 a.m. tomorrow!!!!!!!

Now the *vital* question is, what am I going to wear? The audition is only 22 hours and 37 minutes from now, and I haven't even thought of one single outfit idea.

Right, I am off to rummage though my wardrobe. *Byeeeeeeee!!!!!*

<u>Friday the 8th of April,</u> standing in the town hall waiting to get auditioned.

We have been waiting here for maybe one whole hour, and the excitement is actually feel-able (Tilda says the word is *palpable* but I'm sure that's more something to do with your heartbeat). Okay, I will write in here with all the info.

Well, to quickly catch you up, the first thing that happened was, Jules came over and Tilda got dropped round mine at 9.15 a.m., so that we could walk down to the audition together. I had about 8 different outfits set out on my bed, and I was in a panic not knowing which one looked the most professional and yet also creative. In the end I chose this:

Wide belt

Chunky jewel necklace

My fave boots

Cool layers

Denim
skirt

We were all jangling about with nerves and
excitement and Jules was also jangling with the
many bangles she was wearing, so I made us all
some coffee to calm us down. I have decided to
start drinking coffee and I am waiting for the
chance to say to a lush boy, "Hey, let's go for a
coffee." That sounds so cool, like you are in New
York where *Friends* is set, instead of in our town,

which is the Middle of Nowhere. Like, in New York you can ask for a

DOUBLE MOCHA SKINNY SOYA latte WITH NON-FAT EXTRA whip HOLD-THE-MACCHIATO

or whatever. But here it's like, "Coffee, please. As in not tea."

Strangely the coffee didn't calm us down but instead it seemed to make us even more hyper. After a final application of Quick-Slick Waterproof Mascara and a sweep of Burnt Sand Eye Enhancer, and a cheese sandwich for Jules who didn't get any breakfast because Benito and Benita ate all the

Frosties to get the mini-Power Ranger out of the bottom of the packet, we were off.

After a bit of waiting in the lobby, a lady came out of the main hall bit with a clipboard and shouted, "I'm the Assistant Casting Director, Ramona Blunt." (She didn't need to say her name – we could tell who it was from the dog-trainer-ish voice!) Then she barked out, "Right, could all the hopefuls file in, please. Please note that if you are under 18 and are chosen we will have to confirm parental consent."

I am a very hopeful hopeful, but Jules is the most hopeful hopeful, because of her drama classes and being all Spanishly fiery and passionate. Tilda is not letting herself be a very hopeful hopeful because she's so shy she doesn't think she'll get picked. If we hadn't gone onstage in the schools' Battle of the Bands concert for charity, she wouldn't have got un-shy enough to even walk through this actual door today.

We got put in Group F, which is for 12 to 18s.

There is this person I know in our group, you will never guess who, because you would guess he would only want to be in one film and that would be, like, *Star Trek 17: The Return of the Geekoids*.

Answer: Simon Driscott (formerly known as the Prince of Pillockdom before I realized that he is quite funny and okay).

He came up to us, and then I realized he had two of the Geeky Minions with him as well. When they reached us they all made this weird hand signal thing out of *Star Trek* that they think is way cool and Simon Driscott said, "Greetings, Earthlings." So maybe he still has a bit of pillockness left lurking in him after all.

Yay! Group F has just been called. Wish me luck!

I really just want to write what happened today straight out in two sentences 'cos it is *sooooooo* exciting, but I will make myself put down all the details in the right order in case future brainy people want to study this journal to find out *How We Used To Live*, like when we did the Victorians at school.

So, Group F went in and there was a panel of three people behind a table. Ramona Blunt was the first one, and we had to give her our names and check she had our addresses right on her list. Then we had to shake hands with the two men and say hello and introduce ourselves, like going, "I'm Lucy Jessica Hartley, nice to meet you." They were called Patrick Moran, who is the director, and Someone Else, whose name I didn't catch because he's American and the accent confused me so that

I forgot to listen. We thought that then we'd have an audition, like doing improvisations of a tree growing or something like in drama lessons at school, but Ramona Blunt just said to wait outside and that was IT.

After a while all the groups got called back into the hall together, and Ramona Blunt said, "Thank you for sparing the time to come today. Obviously I can't cast you all, and if you don't get in, please don't be disheartened. Our choices are largely based on age and looks."

Then she read out names of people from Groups A to E, which seemed to go by in a flash, 'cos they were only calling about 4 from each group. Being grown-ups, the ones who hadn't got in all went "Well done, good effort" to the ones that had, like they didn't mind for themselves. Then it came to Group F —

Dun-dun-dun!

Me and Jules and Tilda all held hands like they do on *Pop Idol*, waiting to hear. It got announced that Simon Driscott is going to be Swain 2, whatever that means. The two Geeky Minions didn't get in, so I don't know what he is going to do without them on the set. They did this hand-shaking "Well done, good try" thing and patted each other on the backs, which was *Extremely Mature* for very-nearly-teenagers.

Amazing news next! Tilda is going to be Milkmaid 1! As in the top milkmaid! She did a big whoop and cheer, which is very un-Tilda-like, and we all hugged in happiness and then me and Jules were waiting excitedly to find out what our parts would be, because we knew if shy Tilda had got in then we definitely had. But we weren't given parts as milkmaids or even serving wenches.

We weren't given parts as anything!

OH NO, you are thinking. So were we.

Then Ramona Blunt was reading out the list of urchins, so we knew she'd gone on to the 7 to 11 age group and that was it. My stomach plummeted into my shoes and Jules shouted, "*Noooooo!*"

really loud. Tilda looked **HORRIFIED** that she'd got in without us.

I thought the best thing was to leave before Jules did something bad, like kick a chair, or I did something worse, like start crying in front of everyone, so we were just halfway out the door when I heard, "Lucy Jessica Hartley – Urchin 12."

So I had got in, but as one of the *children*! Typical! I had a suspicion that I needed at least an A cup to be in Group F. Now I'm stuck with the brats because I am a *late developer* as Mum and the assistants in Marks and Sparks bra department call it.

How totally embarrassing!

But at least I had a part! Poor Jules! It was totally awful, 'cos she's the most actressy one of all of us and she wants to do it for an actual career! So we were just all three frozen in *horrification*. But then...

Dun-dun-duuuuuunnnnn!

↖ suspenseful music

It was as if the *Hand of Fate* took over and Ramona Blunt barked out, "Could Julietta Perez Garcia Benedicionatorio see me now, please?"

Jules looked startled, and then she went stomping over in a mega-dark and stormy mood about not getting chosen. But when she got back it was a different picture, and she was nearly skipping, with a huge grin on her face!

What happened is, one of the proper actresses has suddenly got ill with *Burning The Candle At Both Ends* (weird name for a virus!) and Jules has got an emergency audition tomorrow for the part of Eliza, the female lead's sister, who is a *Posh Young Lady*.

How completely mind-blowingly, amazingly beyond your wildest dreams and totally fabutastic is that?!!! Plus, Ramona Blunt told Jules who the stars are, which is Caterina di Fablio, the most stylish woman in the world, and the drool-makingly gorgeous Daniel Blake. Me and Tilda were in total **SHOCKED STUNNEDNESS** when

Jules told us that!!! Daniel Blake is normally only in Hollywood and *Celeb* mag, and it is just *astonishing* to think he'll be in our town and we'll be on a film set with him!!!

So we all stumbled out of the town hall and we were just sort of jumping up and down and hugging and squealing with **AMAZEMENT**, when Jules suddenly looked down at her purple-stripey-tightsey-scruffly-bunchly self and wailed, "Oh no! I've got to audition for the part of a *Posh Young Lady*, and I don't know how to be one! I don't know anything about the manners or the clothes or how you're meant to stand or *anything*!"

Jules looked utterly stricken with panic, but Tilda just smiled. "Don't worry," she said. "I've read loads of Victorian novels, so I can help you. We can turn you into a *Posh Young Lady* in no time."

In fact, Tilda is right now reading the book that the film is based on, which was actually written in Victorian times. She reckons that the story is basically that Mariah (C. di Fab) falls in love with John the Honest Farmer's Son (D. Blake), but Mariah's father doesn't want her to marry him, because he's a peasant and not posh. In those days posh meant like being a Gentleman, whereas now there are no Gentlemen, and we only use that word to mean the men's loos.

Well, we all had a group hug of happiness, and then we went back to Jules's. Me and Jules made some toast and jam, while Tilda worked out a training programme for Jules to do, like this:

Posh Young Lady Training Programme

1) Deportment
2) Manners
3) Modesty
4) Gifts

I promised Jules I would join in too, so we were the pupils and Tilda was the teacher.

33

1) *Deportment.* I thought this meant getting thrown out of the country like you see happening on the news, but apparently it means how you stand, as in your posture and that. So to learn this we had to walk round the room balancing books on our heads.

BEFORE... AFTER...

2) *Manners.* According to Tilda this is not just "please" and "thank you" and saying "excuse me" after you accidentally do a parp. (Tilda says **PYLs** simply did not do them and that is that.) Instead it is more like being *Gracious And Ladylike At All Times,* like going:

"Ah, Mrs. Bennett, how doth your garden grow! I should very much like to possess the garden that brings forth such abundant blooms." So basically it is talking poshly and not interrupting anyone.

BEFORE...

AFTER...

3) **Modesty**. This one was quite easy because it's just about not showing your ankles, weirdly, or anything above them. The Victorians thought ankles were so rude they covered up table legs and piano legs as well, according to brainy Tilda.

Ooooooohhhhh, saucy – NOT!!!

BEFORE...   AFTER...

Unmodest   Et voila!   I quickly made
Modest!   this out of towels

4) *Gifts*. Jules thought she was going
to get actual *gifts,* so she was
quite excited, but turns out this
means *talents*, like singing and

dancing and stuff. Tilda said, "Show me what
you can do now," and Jules belted out this rock
song and did this mad moshy dancing. Tilda
said, "Hmm, we have quite a challenge on our
hands, I think." Then she taught us some

Victorian dancing, which is basically walking round the room in a circle looking *Gracious And Ladylike At All Times* and occasionally galloping down the middle with a boy. But not wild galumphing, more like gentle and sedate stepping. It took Jules ages to get it, but in the end she was like:

BEFORE...   AFTER...

Jules said, "That's the dancing sorted, but what about the singing?" Tilda blushed and said, "Maybe we should forget about that for the moment, and if someone on the film set asks you to do it, pretend to have a sore throat."

Tilda is good at being subtle like that, like, if it was me, I would probably have gone, "No offence, but your singing is totally terrible," and then Jules would have got into a dark and stormy with me.

So you can see that the transformation of Jules was amazing, even more amazing than the time I turned her into Julietta the Superswot. Then Jules and me helped Tilda practise her cow milking on a blown-up washing-up glove until Tilda's dad came to get us. He dropped me at home, and Mum and Alex were massively excited about me being in the film, and Mum has done the permission letter so it is all official and definite.

She did say I have to finish all my holiday homework tonight 'cos the filming goes on right up till next Saturday, but I told her I have in fact done the maths and science (amazingly actually

TRUE! thanks to some very boring rainy days at the start of this week when me and Alex were getting looked after by Nan – I mean Delia!). The only bit I've got left to do is this Memory Box thing for English, where we decorate a shoebox and put things in it that remind us of our holiday.

Well, I did the shoebox at Delia's too, and it's really cool. I decorated it like this...

But I haven't got anything to put in it yet 'cos nothing has actually happened. (I could put some rain and homework in it, but then the homework would get ruined and the box would go soggy, so probably not my best thinking ever.) Instead I am going to wait for exciting happenings to occur while I'm being an extra. In fact, I am right now staring at a poster of Daniel Blake that I got out of *Hey Girls!* mag, and imagining what it'll be like to be actually near him in real life!!! Mum also cut this feature out of her *Celeb* mag for me. ⟶

Fabulous *Di Fablio* hooks lead in movie – and gets *hooks* into leading man!

STYLE QUEEN **Caterina di Fablio**, who started this season's three-belt and gypsy skirt trend, has snagged the lead role in Patrick Moran's ***Passionate Indiscretions***, currently filming at various locations in the south-west. Last weekend she was spotted leaving a London nightspot draped around her co-star **Daniel Blake**, the hottest young thing to come out of Hollywood since Leonardo di Caprio. Toy boy Daniel is one in a long line of leading men linked with the star, who has been making movies since she was fifteen. Caterina looks **crazy in love** right now, but will this fling last longer than the filming of their on-screen romance?

Celeb says **Watch This Space!**

Well, I won't have to *Watch This Space*, 'cos I'll be right there to see with my own two eyeballs if their love lasts, won't I? I, Lucy Jessica Hartley, will be at the front line of Hollywood goss! How totally cool is that?!!

In fact there is so much to be mega-excited about I have made an actual list.

 ☆ **Things To Be Mega-Excited About** ☆

1) Seeing Daniel Blake in real life and getting to be in the same film as him.
2) Seeing Caterina di Fablio in real life and asking her where she gets all her great style ideas from.
3) Daniel Blake and Caterina di Fablio admiring the cool outfit I am putting together to wear on the first day of filming.
4) Me and Tilda being extras in a movie that loads of people will go and watch at the actual cinema with popcorn and everything!

5) Jules maybe getting a proper part in the film that will maybe lead to a career as an actress and will maybe make her rich and famous and will maybe end up with her letting me and Tilda ride round in her black limo with a TV in the back and...

Okay, so that's a lot of maybes, and maybe I'm getting a bit carried away, but it's fun to dream!

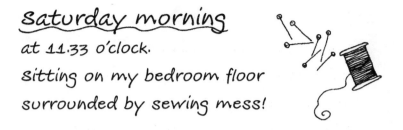

<u>Saturday morning</u>

at 11.33 o'clock.

Sitting on my bedroom floor surrounded by sewing mess!

When I first woke up this morning I was so excited about being in the

film

I just bounced straight out of bed and got ready. Jules is right this minute at her audition (her mum took her there), and I have been keeping my fingers crossed for her all morning (even though that made it quite hard to have a shower and eat my cereal!). I have also done a good luck spell from my Teen Witch Kit, which was ⎯⎯⎯→

Good Luck Spell

To bring good luck to yourself or a friend,
you'll need three cinnamon sticks and a long piece
of red ribbon. First of all close your eyes and take
three deep cleansing breaths. Then imagine the
person to whom you wish to bring good luck.
See them clearly, achieving the thing they desire
and looking very happy. As you do this, slowly bind
the sticks together with the ribbon and tie the ends
in a neat bow. Then put the bundle on your
mantelpiece and every time you see it, send
another good luck wish to your friend.

Hopefully it will work, 'cos Mum is annoyed
with me for using the cinnamon sticks when they
are meant to go in the apple crumble she's making
for tomorrow. She is also annoyed 'cos when I was
focusing on Jules's luck with my eyes closed I got
off balance and knocked into my sewing box and
now there are cotton reels and sequins and

diamantés and needles and bits of material everywhere when she's only just hoovered. So I have had to uncross my fingers to clean up (and quickly write this, obviously!), but they are still crossed in my head.

JULES GOT IN! JULES GOT IN! JULES GOT IN!

so the cinnamon spell worked and it was worth getting in trouble with Mum about the apple crumble!

Oh wow, I cannot believe my **BFF** has got an actual part in the film! She's going to be famous!!! Maybe the black limo thing *will* actually happen in real life!!! Of course, we really wanted to have a jumping-up-and-down-squealing-and-hugging-each-other session, but Jules is going away to a big family Easter party in London that lasts the whole weekend, so we had to make do with screeching madly down the phone. I was so excited when we rang off that I grabbed Mum and Alex and made

46

them do the squealy-huggy-jumping-up-and-down thing with me, even though they didn't actually know what it was for. Then I explained about Jules, and we did it again in happiness for her.

Right, now I'm off to plan my fab film set outfit, especially important now that my **BFF** is going to be an **ACTUAL ACTRESS** and she'll probably introduce me to Daniel Blake *(yum!)* and Caterina di Fablio *(cool!)*.

Easter Day, even though
in my head it is more like
waiting-for-the-film-to-start-
tomorrow day!

Dad brought round these Easter eggs for us this
morning. That made me think of how nice it is
that he stayed in Sherborne instead of going off
round the world to be a roadie, like he planned.
He's now got a job at **WICKED FM**, which is the
local radio station, as their running-around person.
But (thanks to me) he's soon going to become
Creatively Fulfilled by being a DJ, although he
hasn't heard which slot he's getting yet.

My Easter egg was Dairy Milk and Alex got a
Caramel one. His is a bit bigger than mine, but
now I am a very-nearly-teenager about to *star* in,
well, okay, *be* in, a film I didn't bother making
him give me a bit of his so it was fair. That just

shows how *mature* I am becoming.

Dad even got one for Mum, which was an Aero one. It was meant to be for *Building Bridges to Peace* between them and at first it worked, 'cos she said, "Oh goodness, that's very kind of you, Brian, but I don't eat chocolate, I have to watch my figure." *That's a fib – in fact she's got a constant supply of chocolate éclairs in the fridge, but my growing matureness stopped me from mentioning it*

Dad was meant to go, "Oh, you don't need to worry about that," but instead he went, "Well, I noticed you were getting a bit chunky and that's why I got you the Aero one, because it's mainly air."

Mum swiped at him with the Easter egg, going, "The *egg* might be mainly air, Brian, but I bet the *box* could still do some damage, to your head, for example!"

I thought Dad would say sorry then but he just went, "Huh! I won't blooming *bother* next year. So, what's for lunch?"

49

We ate all together, with Delia (my nan, remember?) as well, which was cool, 'cos I got to tell her and Dad all about the film, and Alex got to show them his new made-up karate moves. At the table, Delia was going on and on about how lovely the house looked, and how fabulous the meal was. When she was talking to my mum, she kept saying, "My Wayward Son" to mean Dad, even though he was right there sitting in front of her polishing off all the roast potatoes. Like, Nan (whoops, I mean, Delia) went, "I don't know what My Wayward Son was thinking of by leaving his beautiful family and giving up a secure job, Sue. Maybe I did something wrong when he was a child. Maybe I didn't love him enough."

Mum said, "Don't blame yourself, Delia. No amount of love is enough for some people." And they both gave Dad Looks of Poison.

Dad threw down his napkin and did a gravelly burp while going, "I, er, I think I'll go and have a kick-about with Alex in the garden." (**BTW**, why do grown-ups try to talk through burps instead of just letting them out?!)

So they went outside, but secretly I know Dad thinks he is too artistic and creative for team sports, so it was just to get away from the *womenfolk* (i.e. us).

see, I am already using olden-day language to prepare for the film!

BTW, at first I was *devastated* when Dad **CRUELLY ABANDONED** us, but I am mostly okay now I am used to it. I'm more interested in thinking about the film actually, so that's why I excused myself from the "*Wayward son*" conversation to come up here and write in this journal.

What I want to tell you is that me and Jules and Tilda all had calls late last night asking us to be at this farm just outside town at 7.30 a.m. *Argh!* That is *soooooo* early, even worse than a school day! But I won't care because I'll be on a film set having the most exciting time of my life! This is the outfit I have finally decided on:

Oh, I have to go now. Mum just called up the stairs that we are all going for an Easter walk as a family, even the *Wayward Son*. I am going to wear my Special Occasion high heels to get some practice at walking like a movie star.

Monday the 11th of April,

aka Filming Day! *Yay!*

Time: 11.32 a.m.

Location: Sitting on the extras'
bus waiting to get called on set!!

Total doughnuts scoffed: 3

See, I am learning movie-making
language already!

Sorry I haven't written anything before now, but it has been *Non-stop Excitement* round here and I've only just had time! **BTW,** the extras' bus is this amazingly cool bus that doesn't go anywhere, and instead of normal bus seats in a row it has some tables like on trains and even some sofas at the back. There are also games and drawing things to keep the little kids entertained, and you can bring your food on and eat it here and it's nice and warm and everything. Me, Tilda and Jules have bagsied a sofa and coffee table at the back of the bottom deck and made it into our own private area by pulling this curtain thing across and putting all our stuff out on the table, like our *Hey Girls!* mags and my Teen Witch Kit and that. It is *soooooo* brilliant!

Tilda's dad collected me and Jules from mine and then dropped us all off here at 7.20 a.m., before driving up to London for some work thing he had to do. By "here" I mean this farm just outside the town, **BTW**. We signed in, then wandered round the trailers and watched the camera people setting up and just felt totally cool. It was fab wearing my brill outfit but I'm not wearing it any more – *boo!* – *hiss!* – and in a minute you'll find out why.

At 8.07 me and Tilda got sent to Costume Van 2, and Jules got sent to Costume Van 1, probably because she has a proper part. Then we had to wait in a line to get into the van, and when we finally did, Tilda got the most amazing milkmaid costume with its own corsety bit and everything. This girl Sophie who was helping her put it on kept going "Deep breath in" and "More" and "A bit more" until Tilda said she was going to faint. But it did give her the most cool *Heaving Bosom*. Then Sophie put the dress on over it and measured round her a bit and pinned it up. Then she took it off and Tilda got sent to Make-up in a cool film-star-ish dressing gown while they did the alterations.

I was really excited by then because I thought I was going to get a *Heaving Bosom* too, which would have been worth the whole nearly-fainting thing. But URGH!!! you will not BELIEVE what I've got to wear. I want to drop dead of mortification!!! When I said I was Urchin 12, Sophie looked on her clipboard and went riffling through the racks and got out this – well, billowy white *nightie* is the only way to describe it.

Sophie looked at me, then at the costume, and then she frowned, so I got excited thinking it was the wrong one and I was going to get a corsety thing instead. But in fact she took it out the door, threw it in the dirt and jumped up and down on it!

Then she smiled and said, "That's better. Togs off and arms up, Lucy."

I firstly checked no one from the queue was peeking into the van (like boys!), then I got undressed down to my knickers and Sophie pulled the shift thing over my head. Then she put my own fab clothes on the hanger and back on the rack. I felt sad for them, just hanging there, when they could have been making me look cool.

I was waiting around for some groovy peasant shoes like Tilda got, but Sophie said, "That's it. Now off you pop into Make-up to get some dirt smeared over your face."

Great! **NOT!**

When I got there Tilda was sitting in an actual make-up chair with two people fussing round her, blusher-brushing some big rosy cheeks on her and re-doing her plaits. I just ended up in a line with the other urchins getting dirt smudged on my face by this bored-looking boy who was probably on work experience.

Tilda called across that I looked cool and I yelled back, "Yeah, right! My costume is just basically a billowy white nightie and dirty feet, while you are getting a *Heaving Bosom*!"

Tilda's rosy cheeks went even redder with blushing then! Plus, it made *Mr. Work Experience* go, "Oh yeah, feet up here, please. I forgot." And he splashed this gross slushy stuff that looked like mud and pig poo all up my legs too.

CRINGE!!!

So *not* a great start to my movie stardom after all.

Tilda got called back in to get her costume, which looked completely amazing. Because she is such a cool **BFF** I tried my hardest not to be jealous, which was tricky because of her having the Heaving Bosom, while I was just billowing boringly like a one-woman washing line.

There was still no sign of Jules, so me and Tilda went to the catering van, where they give you stuff like doughnuts and bacon sandwiches, which Mum would never let me have for breakfast normally, because she believes in High Fibre.

We were hoping to see Daniel Blake and Caterina di Fablio in the queue, but they seemed to be getting stuff specially delivered to their trailers. In fact, they probably get whatever they want like a fruit basket with a huge pineapple in the middle or tubes of Smarties with all the yellow ones taken out or something. When I am a famoso fashion designer and I am shooting adverts on location for my Fashion Empire, I will come and eat doughnuts and bacon sandwiches like everyone else, to show I have not become all starry.

Finally Jules emerged out of Costume Van 1, looking *soooooo* not like Jules at all! This is my picture of why (that I did on a napkin during some of the waiting):

Ringlets

Pouty
make-up

Heaving
Bosom (not

Cool corset

Frills and
flounces

Cute lacy-up
boots (also

Plus, she was doing all the *Posh Young Lady* things that Tilda taught her yesterday, like standing up straight and covering her ankles. Apparently she was in there all that time getting taught how to sit down in the dress in a ladylike way by Meg, the head costume lady. Jules reckons if you don't practise how to do that your skirt flips up and shows your pants, which is definitely not a PYL thing!

She was also gabbling at 45 miles an hour, going, "You won't believe this! I've just been briefed on my first scene and I'm going to be in the carriage that drives past the farmyard. I'm going to be in there with Caterina di Fablio!! It's the first time her character notices *John the Honest Farmer's Son*, who is being played by Daniel Blake!! Can you believe I'm going to be in a carriage with Caterina di Fablio, looking out at Daniel Blake?!"

After Jules told us that, me and Tilda were just in a daze of thinking **WOW** that our **BFF** will be acting with such massively sparkly shiny stars! I was also feeling a tiny-weeny bit green with envy to be honest, because Jules gets to goggle at Daniel Blake out of a carriage, when I am too embarrassed to go anywhere near him in this revolting nightie thing.

Of course, I would never tell Jules my feelings in a million years, and we were just having a celebration **BFF** hug, when Todd, who is the person in charge of the extras, yelled at me to come away from her because she isn't allowed to get dirty. Todd was the American man at the audition. He's not in charge of Jules herself because she's not an extra but a proper actress. This nice smiley blonde lady called Laura is in charge of Jules instead, and she just now came on the bus to check if Jules is okay and if she needs anything (Jules is allowed to go on the actors' bus, but she wanted to sit with us instead). We wanted to get Jules to ask for ~~Twixs~~ ~~Twixes~~ ~~Twix's~~ a Twix each for all of us, but we don't dare because of the Professional Attitude thing meaning not being demanding.

Oh, yeah, so then Simon Driscott came up to us in his Swain 2 costume, which is like this:

Can you believe they even made him special victorian shape glasses?

They have made Simon's hair Victorian for the film, but weirdly that makes it look more trendy than normal!

He said to me and Tilda, "Felicitations, ladies."

Tilda went, "Hello," and I mumbled, "Hi."

I felt totally embarrassed being Urchin 12, even just in front of Simon Driscott, so like, how would I feel if a cool boy was here, like who I fancied or something?

63

"Ah, thou must be a milking wench, yon Miss Matilda-Jane," he went then, and I was thinking "*Huh?*" but he just said to me, "And Miss Lucy is become a poor peasant pauper, begging in th'streets for a ha'penny for to buy gruel or a night at t'workhouse."

I was just about to go, "*Grrr!* Why can't you talk in English instead of Victorian?" when Jules said, "Hello? I'm standing right here, you know! Sheesh! It's a sad day when the Prince of Pillockdom thinks he's too cool to talk to me!"

I nudged Jules hard for calling him the P of P. Simon didn't seem to mind, though. He just did this exaggerated double take with stepping back and everything and went, "Why, Julietta! I recognized you not in your finery, so unlike yourself do you appear! You look radiant, divine — instead of resembling an avenging hell demon as is your customary wont."

I was still going, "Huh?" when Jules went, "Shut up, okay! It's not my style but I have to wear it because I'm going *in* a carriage with Caterina di Fablio and being a proper actress! And just because I'm a  now doesn't mean I will be at home time, so watch out!!"

Simon just grinned and bowed, going: "Whatever m'lady wishes, for I am just a simple swain, and I know my place."

Oh, we've just been called on set. Gotta go!

Well, when we got on set, Todd yelled at us what we had to do, so we all knew *our* places, which are called our "marks", and we all had to listen carefully while the director (called Patrick Moran, remember?) explained the scene through a loudhailer. He has wild black hair and even wilder movements, like he's had too many coffees. I am supposed to run across the farmyard with the urchins, and 'cos I am the oldest urchin I have a special bit of getting to pinch an apple from the basket of this farm woman. How cool is that?!

Tilda has to stride across the yard with her milk buckets and go into the cowshed, but she doesn't have to milk any actual cows, even though there are real ones in there. That is lucky 'cos she's quite scared of how big and lumbery they are.

Jules got ushered away into the carriage by lovely Laura, but Caterina di Fablio didn't appear. Then for ages everyone was just fiddling with cameras and these silver boards, and then, just when we were about to *do* something, they called a break and we all had to go and hang around the catering van again (doughnuts still, and now biscuits and tea as well).

When we were full up with free doughnuts, we got the giggles and made up this waiting song.

Why are we waiting?
We are dehydrating!

We sang that one for a bit, then we tried to think of another one, but we couldn't come up with any rhymes. After a bit of thinking, Tilda made up:

Why are we waiting?
We are respirating!

Tilda reckons that just means breathing, so it is true at least. Well, half true, 'cos Tilda and Jules are hardly respirating at all, because of the corsets, especially after 5 doughnuts each, so at least I have found one advantage of my stupid billowy urchin nightie, even if I do just look like a ghost with a head.

Then we went back to our den on the extras' bus (where I am now) and played *Fantasy Dates With Daniel Blake* (I know he is going out with Caterina but it's fun to dream!). What you do is you write down your ideal Fantasy Dates secretly on bits of paper and then pass them round (but don't read them out loud 'cos Fantasy Dates are secret **BFF** stuff). There was mucho, mucho giggling, and in fact the other milkmaids and swains and urchins kept poking their heads round our curtain and asking us what we were doing, but we still wouldn't tell them!!!

I pretended to go to the portaloos to rip the papers into tiny bits and flush them away, but instead I secretly kept them to stick in here. *(Portaloos are like real loos, but outside, BTW, and with weird blue stuff that comes out when you flush them, instead of normal water.)* Bet you can guess whose is whose!

My fantasy date with Daniel Blake is him taking me to a Fleurs du Mal concert and us getting to stand right up the front, and then going to the party afterwards, and then Daniel introducing me to the whole band, and then them asking me to join!

Goth rocky girl band -
BIG clue!

My 'Fantasy Date' with Daniel Blake is going to a film premiere that he is in and getting out of the limo and then walking down the red carpet thing with all the ~~paparazi~~ ~~paparzi~~ ~~paparazzy~~ s newspaper photographers taking pix of me in my cool dress that has been specially created for me by Stella Boyd, my fave designer. Everyone would be going "Who's that girl?", and the next thing you know I would be in 'Celeb magazine' as Daniel's mysterious new girlfriend and I would move to Hollywood where there are no stricty teachers making you wear your uniform properly and also where they have 28 types of coffee.

> My Fantasy Date with Daniel Blake is not going out with Daniel Blake but with someone who I've got loads in common with and who I actually like as a person, instead of just fancying him because he is a gorgeous Hollywood actor.
> So there!

When me and Jules read that one (you've guessed it — Tilda's!) we were like, "Huh?" and I went, "Oh, please, Tilda, just fancy him as well so that we can be a three! Then we can make up Secret Plans to get noticed by him, which'll be *mega-fabulicious*!"

But Tilda says he is so totally not her type she won't even join in just for fun, and also, that we should be careful not to get too bothered about Daniel Blake because we might get *rivalrous* (I think that's what she said) and fall out about it. We have promised that would never ever happen in a million years (like, *Hello*, we *do* know better than to put a boy in front of our **BFF**ness!!!), but she still won't fancy him with us and that is that.

Then we got called back on set to stand on our marks, and after lots more fiddling with cameras and stuff, the stars appeared!!!

Daniel Blake was even more gorgeous in real life than in mags and films! He stood quite near me and the urchins in the farmyard, and it was really exciting, although I was a bit worried he'd turn round and see me standing there in my awful costume! I was interrupted from staring adoringly by Patrick Moran yelling at us that we weren't allowed to goggle at Daniel, because to us he would be just John the Honest Farmer's son and not a celeb.

Caterina di Fablio also came out, followed by these two girls, who looked like bridesmaids, trailing after her holding her long dress out of the dirt. She was carrying a copy of *Celeb* magazine and wearing some Chanel sunglasses even though it was completely cloudy.

71

Jules told me afterwards that Caterina di Fablio didn't speak a word to her in the carriage at first, but instead she just flipped through her magazine and muttered about other celebs, like going, "There's no way she's lost weight! She slaps on some slimming leg make-up and gets in *Celeb* magazine, whereas I lose a stone on the watermelon diet and look fabulous but not one single pap turns up! Typical!" Then she suddenly pulled off the sunglasses and stared at Jules like she had been talking to her all along, so Jules quickly went, "Yeah, completely unfair!", and then Caterina di Fablio smiled.

Now they are like **BFF** apparently, but not actual **BFF** of course because Caterina di Fablio has got Jennifer Aniston and Kate Winslet and Jules has got me and Tilda.

The first time they did the *take* (which means actually filming the scene instead of just rehearsing) poor Jules got yelled at embarrassingly through the megaphone by Patrick Moran, 'cos she was supposed to be looking out of the carriage window *disdainfully* at the general scruffiness below her, but instead, as soon as she saw Daniel Blake, she grinned hugely and couldn't take her eyes off him. Only Caterina di Fablio's eyes are supposed to be on Daniel. They are supposed to have a lingering look and then that is it – **BANG** – *Forbidden Love*. So they had to do it again with Jules looking *disdainful*. She had no problem that time 'cos being yelled at had put her in a huge sulk!

I don't know why the director made a big deal about Jules 'cos in the end we had to do the scene over and over again about a zillion times anyway, but who can possibly understand the minds of creative people with wild hair???

Tilda did a good job walking across the yard with her buckets, and my apple-pinching bit went okay, but unfortunately Mr. Wildhair (my new name for Patrick Moran) told the urchins to be waggish and laugh and shout a lot. In fact they have given me a migraine. I'm not sure how that's different from a normal headache apart from it's what you get when annoying twerps are stressing you out. I am hereby officially renaming them the Awful Urchins.

At the moment, Jules is busy listening to her iPod and Tilda is reading these big heavy books like –

I invented that one but you get what I mean

I'm angling this journal away from them just in case, though, 'cos I'm going to write something I probably shouldn't, which is

→ Oh it's *soooooo* unfair that Jules got to look at Daniel, and he got to see her in her fab costume, and so unfair that Jules and Tilda both look so great and grown-up when I look like a tiny foetus (which means so young you are not even born yet!). I don't want them to read this 'cos it's not their fault, but still, if jealousy really did make you turn green I would be looking like a big bag of limes right now!

Date: **Tuesday the 12th.**

Time: 8.42 a.m. (yaaaaawn!)
Location: On the film set
(how cool does that sound?!)
Total doughnuts scoffed: 2

Well, this morning I am back here again wearing my delightful (**NOT!**) billowy nightie thing. We are hanging out on the extras' bus doing the quizzes in **Hey Girls!** while making friendship bracelets. Also, Tilda has come up with a **Secret Plan** to help Jules get noticed by Daniel, which is to do pretend fainting at his feet. Tilda reckons the **Posh Young Ladies** in her Victorian novels are always doing it.

When they first said about it I got a bit grumpy and Jules said, "Don't worry, Lu, we can make a plan up for you as well," but I grumbled that there is no way I want Daniel to notice me while I am wearing this ~~monsterosity~~ ~~monsterity~~ ~~munstosity~~ gross costume, but only once I'm in my cool gear at home time.

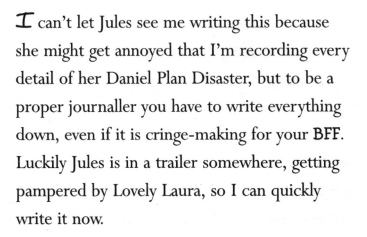

I can't let Jules see me writing this because she might get annoyed that I'm recording every detail of her Daniel Plan Disaster, but to be a proper journaller you have to write everything down, even if it is cringe-making for your **BFF**. Luckily Jules is in a trailer somewhere, getting pampered by Lovely Laura, so I can quickly write it now.

☆ The Daniel Plan ☆ Disaster

1) First of all, Jules fell right down at Daniel's feet, going

This is what you say when you are fainting, BTW

swoon!

It was really believable, but Daniel just stepped **RIGHT OVER** her and carried on walking along with Caterina di Fablio and drinking his coffee.

2) Jules got really determined then, because the one thing she's definitely not is a giver-upper. So she hurried round in front of Daniel and got a bit of a run-up, then crashed straight into him, **THEN** fainted.

3) According to Tilda, Daniel was supposed to catch Jules in his arms and it would be *Instant Love*. Instead, he leapt backwards

and cursed in American as his coffee slopped all down him, and Jules went slithering to the floor.

4) Caterina di Fablio had a big scream at Jules, saying how stupid and clumsy she was. Jules was lying on the floor with her eyes shut and for all C. di Fab knew, she could have been needing *Urgent Medical Attention*. This has made us three go completely off C. di Fab as both a *Style Icon* and a *Human Being* and from now on I will not be copying that thing she does with three belts and the gypsy skirt, even if it *is* set to be the summer's hottest trend!

5) Daniel **FINALLY** realized Jules was unwell and shouted:

"Hey, swain-boy, handle this, will you?"

6) Unfortunately for Jules the swain-boy he was talking to was in fact Simon Driscott. Daniel wandered off and Simon Driscott instantly started loosening Jules's corset and she shouted:

7) Simon Driscott looked really freaked out and went:

8) Jules hissed at Simon:

I'm trying to get Daniel's attention, all right? So make it look serious!

Then she quickly fell down in her faint again before Daniel could notice the *Miraculous Recovery*.

9) Simon Driscott really got into the acting thing then, like:

Help! Serious incident over here, we're looking at a pulmonary embolism or cardiac arrest! She's crashing! She's crashing!

I think it must have been stuff he heard off ER or more likely a quite medical episode of Star Trek

10) Daniel still didn't even notice 'cos he was miles away by then, so eventually Jules gave me and Tilda an eye-rolling look and that was the end of the Daniel Plan.

To be honest I was secretly a tiny bit glad, because I didn't really want Jules to get noticed by Daniel when I fancy him as well. She is already getting to be a star when I am blending into the background like boring wallpaper.

Now I feel bad about writing that, but it's in pen so I can't even rub it out. Oh, *boo! Hiss!* Nothing is going right for me today!!!

It's definitely one of those irony things we did in English that I **WANTED** Daniel to notice me, but now I've got this awful costume I'm hoping he **WON'T** in actual fact!

Oh, we have been called on set, **Yay!**

<u>I wish we hadn't
been called on set after all!</u>

Oh dear – Daniel Blake has definitely noticed me
now, but not in a good way! I have just had a giant
attack of **CRINGITIS** right in front of him, and so
I have written a letter about it to *Hey Girls!*
magazine for the *Readers' Most Embarrassing
Moments* page. But I haven't decided yet if I'm
posting it or not. Some things are maybe too
embarrassing to even send in to your fave mag.

If there's still a letter here when you read this,
and not a blank space, you'll know I didn't dare
send it in after all!

83

Dear Hey Girls! magazine,

I was the winner of your Fantasy Fashion Comp (Hi, Alicia!), and also I am a keen reader of your Readers' Most Embarrassing Moments page. Recently I sent in a Reader's Most Embarrassing Moment, but you didn't print it because it was over 100 words (in fact it was 716). But remember you said to write in again when something the same amount of embarrassing or more embarrassing happened? Well, it has now happened, and so I am doing what you suggested.

My Reader's Most Embarrassing Moment is...

I am at this exact second working on a film as an extra. My two BFF have got these really cool costumes with actual corsets that give them Heaving Bosoms, but I have got stuck with a white billowy nightie thing because I am Urchin 12, which is the oldest urchin, but still lumped in with the children basically, even though I am a very-nearly-teenager. So today for once I was in the front near the camera and this evil gust of wind blew right up my billowing nightie thing, and it went flying up to nearly over my head, and the whole entire WORLD saw my knickers, including DANIEL BLAKE. Yes, as in <u>the</u> Daniel Blake. As in Daniel Blake who <u>Celeb</u> magazine called "the hottest young thing to come out of Hollywood

since Leonardo di Caprio" has seen my pants.
Even WORSE (if that is humanly possible!) they
were these embarrassing frilly ones Nan bought
me that I only wear if there are absolutely no
other ones left in my drawer. As you can guess I
was <u>mortified</u> (as in so embarrassed I wanted to
drop down actually dead).

So triple-please print this RMEM to warn other
girls about the dangers of billowingness! I
know it is actually 191 words, but it was far
too embarrassing to fit into only 100, so
hopefully you will still print it anyway.
Yours fingers-crossedly,
Lucy Jessica Hartley xxx

Yikes! I cannot believe Daniel
Blake saw my knickers!!! My
cheeks are glowing bright red and
I am burning with shame every time
I even think about it! Now I have got to make him
notice me in a **GOOD WAY** so it will undo the
CRINGE-MAKING image in his head! I will also
have to solve this awful-costume dilemma before
my reputation as Style Queen goes entirely out of
the window.

Oh, hang on, I think a *Secret Plan* is coming
into my head.

Time: 6.03 p.m., after a
nice bubbly bath with fash mags.
Brilliant Secret Plans: 1 (shhhh!!!)
Total doughnuts scoffed: 6
(and I managed to nab
one to bring back for Alex too.)

Just on the way out tonight we got given these!

To thank you for all your hard work,
Cherry Pip Productions
would like to invite you to a

Wrap Party

at the Eagle Hotel, Sherborne
on Saturday 16 April from 7.30 p.m.
Black tie optional. Style essential.

(Under 18s must be accompanied by an adult.
Parents and siblings welcome.)

How totally cool is that?!!! I'm going to put together a really glammy and film-star-ish outfit for it, maybe even with long gloves and everything, you know the kind you wear big diamond rings over, like ⟶

Mum is nearly as madly excited as I am and is right now rummaging through her wardrobe to find her Ghost dress that used to be new and is now vintage. I'm not sure if Dad will come, though. I don't think he has a black tie. In fact, I think the only one he owns is turquoise with Bart Simpsons all over it. And if *style* is *Essential* then he's definitely in trouble. Still, I will ask him because I have asked Mum. You have to make sure things are fair between parents otherwise they get cross and fall out with each other.

At first I got really excited thinking Daniel Blake would be at the party and see me in my glammy dress and the gloves and that, but Jules said she thinks the main stars will be way too important to bother with a party in Sherborne but will probably go to a cool nightclub in London instead. Oh well, it's still a fab excuse to get dressed up, especially after a week spent walking around in a modified bedsheet with pig poo smeared up my legs!

Okay, talking of my vile costume, now it's time to tell you my *Secret Plan*. Basically, I have got the most *fantablious* idea to look cool like Jules and Tilda on the film set instead of like a small child. My plan is so great that I had to invent the new word of *fantablious* to describe it. I steered clear of the Awful Urchins as much as possible today so I don't have to go to bed early with a cold flannel over my face because of a migraine. This is lucky because I will probably stay up almost all night to do my plan, which is…

Oh, no, actually it's so secret I can't even write it down in here…yet…but let me just give you a private clue.

When I got changed back into my normal clothes this afternoon I sort of accidentally on purpose forgot to hang my billowy white nightie thing back up and kind of ended up bringing it home with me in my bag. Whoopsie!

Clue

So maybe you can guess what I am in fact up to.

If not, I promise I'll tell you tomorrow when I've finished!

Gotta go now and start it. *Byeeeeee!*

Tuesday at 2.41 a.m.,
oh, hang on,
that makes it Wednesday.

Urgh! sooooo tired, but must keep going…

Date: Wednesday the 13th.
Time: Way too early.
Location: Sherborne Hall (much more
posh than on the farm!).
Total doughnuts scoffed: 0

I am too tired even to eat a doughnut, in fact the
thought of food makes me feel sick. I think that's
because I only slept for about 2 hours and maybe
31 minutes last night (triple yawn!). Still, it was all
worth it, 'cos I can now unveil my *Secret Plan*. It
is that I have worked nearly all night re-designing my

costume and it looks like this. *(Da-daaaaaaa!!!)*

Mud washed off

Necklace I made out of wire and beads

Hairclip and gorge dangly earrings

Rolled up sleeves

Studded belt

Cool scarves

Inside out

Two gypsy skirts put underneath for volume

My cowboy boots

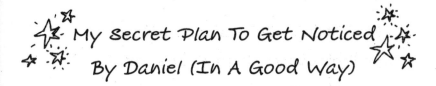

My Secret Plan To Get Noticed By Daniel (In A Good Way)

1) I am secretly wearing my costume right now, but no one can see any of the new design, because it is all hidden on the inside.

2) When you wear it the right way round, it just looks like the usual billowing white nightie thing.

3) I'll only change it round at the very last minute, so no one will notice and make me change it back. All I have to do is turn it inside out, draw in the waist and then add the belt and scarves and gypsy skirts, which are lying in wait in my bag.

4) While Mr. Wildhair is filming, I'll walk past Daniel on set in that model-y way I learned on the catwalk at London Fashion Week. That way he'll notice me AND my cool re-designed costume will be in the film forever!

94

5) Mr. Wildhair will be in amazement and probably change everyone else's outfits to be like mine.

6) Daniel Blake will think...

Wow, that girl is so groovy I'll probably let her become my personal style guru or maybe even my actual girlfriend and take her on her Fantasy Date, which will be exactly like she imagined it, except even better!

And that is how I will get whisked off from the boringness of my life to fashion stardom!

HA-HA-HAAAAAA! ← Evil genius laugh!

Oh, gotta go, it's time to put My Secret Plan To Get Noticed By Daniel (In A Good Way) into action.

Wish me luck!!!

Hiding
in the costume van.

You will not believe the awfulness of just now. I felt sick before from the tiredness, but now I feel completely *vomitacious* like I have swallowed a hedgehog whole. Well, what happened was, I went...

No, I'm too upset to write it down now. Instead I am going to tunnel into this big pile of petticoats and have a massive cry.

Okay, I can write about it now.
It might help get the upsetness out of my brain and down my arm and into this journal. But honestly, right now I feel like I'll be upset forever!

What happened was, we got called and it was time for my big cool on-set appearingness. I quickly whipped behind a haystack and reversed my costume and added the accessories, then got on my mark. As usual I was so far away in the distance that no one noticed the change. When Mr. Wildhair called "Action!" I put *My Secret Plan To Get Noticed By Daniel (In A Good Way)* into action too. So instead of pushing a wheelbarrow of pig poo across the background, I ran up close to the camera and did my model-y walk *right past* Daniel Blake. I was so nervous and hopeful that my heart was hammering really hard in my chest, and I was worried the big fluffy microphone thing would pick up the *dum-dum-dum* sound.

Well luckily it didn't, and the plan was definitely working because Daniel Blake was looking at me in a *mesmerized* way. But then Mr. Wildhair shouted, "Cut!" and started waving wildly at me and bellowing, "You girl, come here!" like Mr. Cain does when I'm trying to sneak past him in the school corridor with a bit of accidental lipgloss and eyeshadow on. Well, I would have been shaking in my boots, if I had any, but instead I was shaking in my bare muddy feet.

I tremblingly walked up to him and he had a total ragey fit, going, "You have wrecked a moment of genius! We'll never recapture it! You've ruined my heavenly take with your ridiculous outfit! I think this film can do with one less urchin. Now **GET OFF MY SET AND DON'T COME BACK!**"

He didn't need to shout that again because I was already bolting off. Jules and Tilda said they really wanted to come after me straight away, but Mr. Wildhair was looking so scary they didn't dare move a minuscule muscle. My head was buzzing, and my stomach was flipping, and my hands were shaking, and I absolutely could not *believe* what had happened. I *really* thought they would all love my costume and be totally impressed. I *really, really* thought it might make Daniel Blake see me as a **V-N-T** (very-nearly-teenager) or even just a T, and not as a tiny infant, and then ask me out on my Fantasy Date. But I was *really, really, really* **WRONG.**

Now I have just got enough of my breath back after crying so much to ring Mum.

At home

Well, luckily Mum came straight away, even though she was in an important meeting with her boss, who is called Mr. Snellerman, and he got annoyed. Mum doesn't dare annoy him usually, because at her work they have been making redundancies (which I have found out are not plastic moulded bits like I thought, but more like getting sacked without doing anything wrong).

After a couple of glasses of wine at the kitchen table with Gloria, Mum once said that Mr. Snellerman is a *Prehistoric Idiot* who doesn't understand the lives of modern working women and if she didn't need the money she'd tell him to put his job where the sun doesn't shine (not sure where that is, exactly, but – maybe in Manchester where it is quite often rainy?). Anyway, she was cross at first with me for phoning, but then when she saw the state of me and heard me gulping out what happened she stopped minding.

I told her why I got chucked out, and I thought she'd be angry, but she just gave me a hug and said, "Oh, Lu, sometimes your creative thinking is a little too creative, that's all. You just misjudged the situation. I can't do anything about the director's decision, I'm afraid, but I'd love to see your creation."

So when we got back here I put it on, and she said it was really good, and she made me twirl around till I went dizzy and then we were both giggling and that's when I started to feel a bit better.

But the B.A.D. news is that there's no way Mum can stay off work and look after me tomorrow (especially with Mr. Snellerman the

Prehistoric Idiot on the warpath), and she *still* won't let me stay at home on my own, even though I am a V-N-T and could do babysitting my actual self! Y-O-Y-O-Y-O-Y is it that everyone else can see your matureness except your own mum? After all, it is only 129 days till I'm actually 13 itself!

I did in fact mention that, but Mum says I have to go on set with Tilda and Jules and just take some things to do and keep out of Mr. Wildhair's way. Nan is away this week, and Alex is round his friend Matthew's, so I begged to go there as well, but Mum says Matthew's mum is doing her a massive favour already by just having *him,* so no. That is a shame 'cos even though hanging out with your little brother is completely embarrassing, it is nowhere near as bad as turning up on a film set you have been chucked off of! Of course, there is no way I can go to the wrap party now either, not when I have completely embarrassed myself in front of everyone. I feel awful about missing out, especially as I had such a good idea for a cool, film-star-ish outfit.

Everything has gone totally wrong today! In fact, I think I'm just going to go to bed now, so nothing else bad can happen.

<u>Date:</u> <u>Thursday the</u>
<u>14th of April.</u>
Not the best day ever in
the life of Lucy Jessica Hartley!!!
<u>Time:</u> Whatever it is, it is moving
veeeeeery veeeeeery slowly.
<u>Location:</u> Well, I am here on the film set,
even though I tried pretending to Mum
that I have doughnut poisoning and
should stay in bed.
<u>Total doughnuts scoffed:</u> 3, 'cos I don't
really have doughnut poisoning at all, and
in fact the doughnuts are now the only
good thing left about being here.

I'm busy trying to hide from Todd so he doesn't
send me home, 'cos then I'd be a real urchin who
has to wander the streets with nowhere to go. Jules
and Tilda have been sneaking me coffee and the
above doughnuts, but mainly they have to keep
away from me or Todd will get suspicious and

come checking round the side of Costume Van 2, which is where I am sitting. I can't even go *in* any of the actual vans, as they are full of busy people.

shhh!!! Quickly writing this in the portaloo on the film set (yes, I am still here!!!)

Sorry this is on actual loo roll, but I didn't want Meg to see me taking my journal into the loo, 'cos I am pretending that the amazing thing that just happened to me is completely normal and happens all the time so that I look cool.

I only have a few minutes to quickly write this, or Meg might think I'm in here doing a you-know-what, which would be completely cringe-making. Oh, hang on, you don't know what I'm on about. Well, I will say it all in bullet points like we use in science for speed and accuracy reasons:

o Meg (the Head of Costume) found me round the side of the costume van.

o I started begging her not to chuck me off the set and explaining about Mum's work and Mr. Snellerman being a Prehistoric Idiot and the redundancies and everything, but she said she is not sending me home, and actually she thought my re-designed costume was great and creative and cool, but maybe not that suitable for a Victorian film.

o She said seeing as I am not in the film any more would I like to help her in her own job of being a wardrobe mistress?

o I went, *squeal!!!!* "I would love that more than being in the film anyway as my one ambition is to be an Actual Real Fashion Designer!" Then I had to hold myself back from hugging her because of having a Professional Attitude.

o   So now I am helping with alterations
    and sewing buttons and brocade onto
    this brilliant dress for the actress playing
    Lady Warwick.

    Wow! Wow! Wow! Now I have got
totally amazing news to tell Mum tonight,
and she won't have to worry about
child~~care~~ very-nearly-teenager care after all!

In bed,

too tired to look at the time but  too excited not to quickly write.

More wow, wow, wows!! What an amazing day!! I have been doing loads of cool stuff like last minute Emergency Ironing and altering hemlines and finding the right-number hangers with the costumes people need for their next scenes by checking the clipboards and that. Plus, there is this scene where *John The Honest Farmer* coughs up blood on a hanky 'cos of being *Not Long For This World*, and they did 13 takes, so I had to keep going on and giving him a new hanky and taking away the one with fake blood all over, which is called *re-setting*. I thought Patrick Moran was going to chuck me off again when he first spotted me, but I just held my head up high and changed over the hankies with such a *Professional Attitude* that he got distracted and started yelling at someone else, so *Phew*!!!

Plus, I am really busy because Meg has given me a...

Special Mission

Set by: Meg

Mission: To design something for one of the extras to actually **WEAR** in the actual **FILM**!!

Brief: (Which is like the instructions to help you do the mission, **BTW**.) The main costumes for the big wedding scene have already been designed, but Meg wants me to make a waistcoat for one of the extras as a special challenge. She says she can't guarantee if they'll use it in the film or not, because for that to happen it would have to be *fabulastically* good. So I have to show her that I can put all the skills and stuff I have learned into action and make it totally, extra specially amazing.

Time: 36 hours, starting from now!

Tick! Tick! Tick!

Time ticking!

There is a lot to think about for my waistcoat design, as well as the actual making and getting the measurements Meg gave me exactly right. I am going to put into use all the stuff I have been learning, like how the material can't be too heavy or it won't move nicely, and how you can't have fine lines or small spots on it or the screen will make it go fuzzy and probably give the audience a migraine. And everything has to be Victorian-y and fit with the times, so like not doing studs for decoration. Plus there is all the emotionality side where you can choose a lively colour to show someone is outgoing, or choose black to show they are shy or maybe a villain. You can match a man's costume's fabric colour to a woman's dress to show their lurve or make it clash to show their enemy-ness.

I have got the design template of a waistcoat to work from, and it is up to me to choose the material from the rolls they've got in the costume van, and the buttons and back-tie buckles and that.

Meg says I can ask anyone else on the wardrobe team for tips too, like Sophie or Becca (Meg's other assistants, who are called *dressers*). But I don't really want to ask them anything 'cos I want it to be all my own work. Plus, I've decided to do it at home in the evenings so I can learn even more on set during the day, like tomorrow we are making fake vomit out of baby food and porridge – how cool is that?!

I have GOT to do a good job and impress Meg so that when I'm older and I am an *Actual Real Fashion Designer* she might employ me to do designing on films.

Dad picked me up today in the end, 'cos Mum got stuck doing extra work for the *Prehistoric Idiot*. Jules directed him to Costume Van 1 and he poked his nose round the doorway. I started burbling out my happy, happy news about how tragedy had turned into *fabulosity* (another word I have made up to mean more fab than the most fabbity-fab thing ever!). Then Dad stepped into the van, banging his head by accident and saying quite a bad swearword. Meg is so cool and great and nice she pretended not to notice that. I was still burbling, but Dad was less listening to me and more staring at Meg while she worked on her sewing machine.

Weird or what?

Maybe he thought he knew her and was trying to think of where from.

I gave up talking then and went, "Dad, Meg, Meg, Dad," in that introduce-y way you do. They shook hands and Dad said, "I'm Brian, actually, when I'm off duty," and Meg smiled.

Then when I was packing up my stuff Dad did this thing of pretending to talk only to me when he knew Meg was listening. I know this because when she put her foot down on the pedal and her sewing machine went clack-clack-clack he talked way louder, even though I was right there by his ear. He said all casualistically, "Oh, Lucy, I've just heard that I'm getting MY OWN RADIO SHOW in a couple of weeks, probably **DRIVE TIME** which is the **MOST POPULAR** slot."

I said, "I know, I was there when you got the phone call, remember?"

Dad gave me a *Look of Poison* (I don't know why) and carried on, going, "It's so great, especially after all the trauma of becoming a **SINGLE MAN** again, and having to cope with being away from my wonderful children."

I was just going, "But it was you who decided to **CRUELLY ABANDON** us and go to live at Uncle Ken's and watch your pants drying on the radiator while strumming your—" But Dad cut me off, shouting out, "Right then, better get going!" and bundling me out of the van. Adults are weird, especially my own particular dad, who is sometimes a *Complete Mystery*.

Oh, look, I am rambling on again! Right – I am *sooooooo* going to sleep this actual second 'cos I've got a whole brilliant busy day of working with Meg tomorrow! She is so amazing and lovely! She…

No, stop right there! I mustn't get distracted from my ZZZZZZs.

Good night!

Friday the 15th

at 8.30 o'clock in the morning.
I am so excited I have
just sprung out of bed
like a kangaroo riding a pogo stick!

We are shooting at Sherborne Hall again today, which is this amazing big posh country house, and even better I am spending the whole day working with the *fantablious* Meg. This could turn out to be the best day ever in my whole entire life so far!

10.29 a.m.,
just having a break
and an apple...

I can't eat one single
doughnut more – urgh! Now
I think I really <u>have</u> got
doughnut poisoning!

...and writing down that Jules just came in here waving her notes for today and shrieking (which she thinks is very girly and usually never does).

When she finally got enough breath to speak, her words came out all jumbly with excitement, like, "There's a bit here where Eliza has this thing with *Hohn the Jonest Sarmer's Fun*! She's outside Herborne Shall, which is her big mansion house, and he comes a-calling on Mariah and they have this Golen Stance."

I went, "Do you mean Stolen Glance?" and Jules nodded.

I was not getting it, though. I was more like going, "But *John the Honest Farmer's Son* is in love with Mariah, so why would he do a Stolen Glance at Eliza?"

Jules went, "It's supposed to show he's a bit of

115

a cad, that's what Tilda reckons."

I didn't get what that was, so she said, "Oh, come on, Lu! A cad is like a bounder or rascal or rapscallion!"

But I didn't get what they were either, so then she said, "It's a bit like Wayne Roman-type boys who have *Wandering Eyes* and like lots of girls at once."

I sure got it then, because of my actual real-life experience when I fell in *Forbidden Love* with Wayne Roman and he pretended to feel the same about me when he was already going out with this girl Tamsin, who has a gross foundation line round her neck.

By this time, Jules had got totally overcome with excitement, like PYLs did in Victorian times. But instead of having to lie down in a dark room and sniff smelly salts, she did a screeching cheering happy dance and shouted, "I am being in a scene with Daniel Blake, and he is giving me a *Stolen Glance*!!! I've got another chance to impress him and there is no way I'm letting it go wrong this time – **NO WAY!**"

So that is lucky for Jules, but what chance will I ever have to impress Daniel now I'm not even in the film? Of course, I love being here with Meg, and all the stuff I'm learning is really cool but I just wish I could find a way to get near him. Time is running out 'cos tomorrow is our final day of filming (this is the last location the crew are shooting at), and then he'll go back to Hollywood, and I'll go back to school, and that will be IT.

Today has taken a turn
for the weird and also
the unexpected.

I am sitting here in an actual chair, one of those
foldy directors' ones, and sipping an orange juice
while writing this. This is because something
AWFUL has occurred, but out of it has come
something QUITE GOOD.

What happened was that Jules was in her PYL
costume and ringletty hair and that, sitting on the
gate looking *fabulisimo*, about to do her *stolen
Glance* scene with Daniel Blake. It took the crew
ages to get set up, and me and Meg were by the
side 'cos we were in charge of any last-minute
costume tweaks. Tilda was with us 'cos she wasn't
in the scene, and so she was just watching. Daniel
finally came on, and after getting fussed over by
the make-up girls, he stood on his mark.
Everything was all ready to go, but then he took a

long peering look at Jules and went, "This is that crazy girl who poured hot coffee over me! Are you sure about her having such a big scene, Patrick?"

Jules looked just as panicked as me and Tilda did. She cried, "I'm so sorry about that. It was a total accident, I promise!"

Daniel sighed and went, "Well, I guess so long as there are no more *accidents*, we'll be okay." But he said it like he didn't believe for one minute that the fainting and coffee-spilling thing was an accident in the first place.

We all three sighed then with massive relief, and Jules went, "Oh no, of course not. I promise there won't be. I have a completely *Professional Attitude*."

And Daniel said, "Okay then, Patrick, let's roll."

But Patrick Moran was looking furiously at Jules and saying, "I didn't know there was an incident—" Jules quickly butted in, clapping her hands and going, "You heard the man, Patrick, let's roll."

Patrick Moran gave her a narrow-eyed kind of look and mumbled warningly, "Fine. But no more second chances." Then he called, "Action," and I was thinking *phew!* she got away with it.

But then disaster struck. They were just about to do the *Stolen Glance* when I spotted that a camera lead was caught on a brick. *So what?* you are probably thinking. But that brick was the brick that was holding the gate in place. Before I could even shout "Stop!", the camera moved on its tracks and the lead tugged the brick out from under the gate and the whole thing, including Jules, started swinging forward. Jules was clinging on and looking completely *horrified*. Daniel was also looking *horrified* 'cos with Jules's weight on it, the gate was moving towards him and then – most *horrifying* of *horrors* – Jules smashed right into him.

"*Oooooofffff!!!!*" he went, folding in half and staggering completely backwards.

"Sorry, sorry, sorry!" Jules was shouting, almost in tears. But Daniel Blake ignored her.

"That girl is **CRAZY**!" he yelled. "If you don't get rid of her, Patrick, I'm going back to L.A. right now!"

So the next thing was, all these assistants came out and had to do *Ego Massaging* on Daniel to make him not go back to America.

And then, even more *horrifying horrific horribleness* happened, 'cos Patrick Moran had a big yell at Jules and said they'd have to get a new actress to play Eliza and re-shoot the earlier scenes with a replacement 'cos Jules was **FIRED**!

Then everyone was having a panic wondering what to do as there is no way they had time to go back and re-shoot those scenes. Jules was trying to say it was an accident, which it truly was, 'cos I saw it with my own eyes, but no one was listening.

And I was thinking, *Eeeeekkkkkk!!!!! I have to have an idea right this second to save Jules's part in the film or she will be devastated forever and ever.* I could see Tilda was thinking that too, but nothing was coming into our brains. And then suddenly like a flash of lightning, or a light bulb coming on, there it was →

Without even thinking of my own safety I marched straight up to Patrick Moran and said, "You could just make it a different person who Daniel has the *Stolen Glance* with on the gate. It doesn't have to be Mariah's sister but just a friend or a maid or something. Then you can leave everything else as it is already. And Jules is only in one more scene, which is the big wedding finale, so you could just put her at the back or something."

Then I stopped talking and I thought Mr. Wildhair was going to start yelling at me not to be so stupid but instead he was saying, "Fine. Go and get changed **RIGHT NOW!**"

I absolutely froze to the spot then, and I was gaping at him and thinking, *What?* Of course I didn't mean **ME** my actual self should have the *Stolen Glance*, but I didn't dare complain 'cos what if he got mad at me again and wouldn't let me work with Meg any more?

Jules looked really upset about Patrick Moran being so unfair, and Tilda rushed over to comfort her. I tried to go too, but Meg said there was no time and hurried me away to the costume van.

After I got over the shock of being back in the film, I felt quite excited. It was *soooooo* cool getting fitted into my costume and it was fab finally wearing something nice, after all that suffering in my stupid white nightie thing! Jules and Tilda are right about the *not being that able to breathe in corsets* thing but I don't care 'cos I have finally **FINALLY** got some you-know-whats. Okay, so they are not a *Heaving Bosom*, but they are a start.

It was so great having my professional make-up done and all my hair ringletted up. In the end I looked totally like a **PYL**.

Then it was time to go on set and I remembered all the **PYL** stuff Tilda had taught Jules and soon I was *awash* with *victorianity*. My stomach was also awash with butterflies because Daniel Blake would finally be noticing me in a good way!

So I sat on the gate and we did the *stolen Glance* scene, and it was really, really cool, especially to be actually near the camera so people will see my face on screen, instead of just my vague shape billowing in the background like a mainsail in a March wind. Daniel was looking at me in a totally fancying way, and I was looking back at him in that way too (I didn't even have to act!), and it was completely amazing and absolutely the best moment of my life so far.

Excuse me while I just stop here and think about it for a while.

Weirdly, Simon Driscott was supposed to be toiling outside in the garden, being swain-like, but when he saw it was me on the gate and not Jules he did this sort of staring, gaping thing and dropped his hoe. Maybe it was because he only half recognized me in all my cool *Victorianosity*.

So now my 4 seconds of fame are over, but I don't mind because I will have them on film forever and ever and loads of people will get to see Daniel Blake looking at me in a fancying way and me having a cool corsety costume and an actual Heaving Bosom (well, kind of). Plus, I am getting to sit in comfort sipping an orange juice, which Lovely Laura has got me, because now I have a proper part she is looking after my every need.

Oh, wait, here comes Jules. She still looks upset about Patrick Moran blaming her for a total accident! Poor Jules – that was *soooooo* unfair of him! But at least I managed to save her from being chucked out of the film altogether. I know, I will cheer her up by telling her how well it went.

Later.

Don't know how much.
Too furious to care!

I am sitting in the little props caravan all on my
own being completely furious. I marched in here
without grabbing my journal, but I have found
some parchment and ink to write with. Sorry if
it's a bit splodgy, but the feather quill thingie is
quite hard to control and plus I am too ANGRY
and UPSET to care about neat writing!!!

Can you believe that Jules is in a mood not
with Patrick Moran but with <u>ME?!</u>

She marched up to me and yelled, "How could
you do that to me?! My Stolen Glance has
become a Stolen Chance, stolen by YOU, Lucy
Jessica Hartley!"

At first I just sat there with my mouth
hanging open, but then I managed to splutter out
about how the only reason I had the idea was to

SAVE her from getting replaced and wiped from the film, and that I never imagined that Patrick Moran would tell ME my actual self to do the Stolen Glance and how I actually thought she should be thanking me!

Jules just stood there with her arms crossed and her nose pointed in the air, and when I stopped talking she did this "Huh!" sound and then went, "Patrick Moran was just about to listen to me saying it was an accident, so you DIDN'T save my part, but you DID steal my best scene, so there!"

And I went, "Well, that is soooooo unfair, 'cos no way was Patrick Moran about to believe you after the Crazy Girl incident with the fake fainting and the hot-coffee spilling!"

Then she said this thing that made me go into total SHOCKED STUNNEDNESS, which was:

"You are not my BFF any more, Lucy Jessica Hartley, and you never will be again, so there!"

And then she stormed off again, and I was so upset that I stormed off too, into this caravan. We have had loads of rows before but she's never said we'll <u>never</u> be BFF again – and I mean NEVER. It's the one forbidden thing BFF should never say, even in the rowdiest of rows. It was sooooooo awful that my stomach keeps flipping over and over, and I feel like being sick.

Have I really lost Jules forever? How can she get this mad when I haven't even done anything? I mean, I didn't ASK to fill in for her. Plus, I deserve a chance to fix Daniel's opinion of me, don't I? I mean, please remember that we are talking about a HOLLYWOOD STAR who has

a) seen my knickers and

b) watched me get yelled at and chucked off set.

In fact, Jules should be PLEASED for me! She just doesn't like it that I've had a Special Moment with Daniel, and she hasn't! Well that's not my fault, is it? Grrrr!

I'm surprised that Tilda hasn't come and found me yet, or at least Simon Driscott, but no, I am still stuck here on my own all alone. I also keep thinking that Jules will come in here and say sorry to me, but she hasn't, not yet. And there's no way I'm saying it first!

Argh!!! We're supposed to be having an amazing time on this film, and instead everything's gone horrible and me and Jules might have broken up forever and ever.

Oh, hang on.

That was Sophie, one of Meg's assistants. She just found me in here and said we're finishing for the day. Oh no, that means I have to have a lift with Jules's mum - well, there's no way I'm talking to Jules for even one minute of the drive home, not when she's just been so completely nasty and unfair to me!

At home –
thank goodness!

As soon as I got home from the horrible journey with Jules, where us two only talked to Isabella (Jules's mum) and not to each other, I went straight up to Mum, and I must have looked v. v. sad, 'cos she pulled me onto her lap without me even saying anything and gave me a cuddle.

I blurted out all the awfulness of how Jules is hating me for getting to do the *Stolen Glance* scene with Daniel instead of thanking me for saving her part.

Mum went, "Well, that's a bit silly, isn't it? I mean, it's only one scene. Why is she so bothered about it?"

So then I had to explain about how Jules has a big crush on Daniel, but I sort of forgot to mention that I do too, and I'm glad I forgot when Mum got all worried and said, "Lucy, I'm very concerned about Jules falling for a 16-year-old film star. Perhaps I should give Isabella a ring."

That completely freaked me out. "Oh, no please don't!" I begged. "Jules will definitely hate me forever if you do that!"

Then I had to convince Mum that Daniel Blake thinks Jules is a *Crazy Girl* and would never ask her out in a gazillion years. Mum gave me a really stern look and said she was trusting me to tell her if that changed even one bit. And I promised I would, which I totally will, if Jules ever even *speaks* to me again. Then Mum stroked my hair and said, "It's such a shame Jules has let a boy come between you two, especially after all your years of friendship."

"I know," I mumbled and came upstairs to write this.

I mean, I understand how she really wanted to do the *Stolen Glance* with Daniel and how the gate thing was an accident so it really wasn't fair she got chucked out of that scene. But then, I was only trying to save her from total chucked-out-ness and complete replacement by someone else, and I didn't know Patrick Moran would make *me* act that part, did I?

Oh, it's all buzzing round and round in my head! I do feel sorry for Jules, but it's so unfair she's taking out her upsetness on me. Why is having **BFF** so difficult sometimes? (If she **IS** still my **BFF**, even.)

Anyway, I absolutely must not think about this even one tiny bit more 'cos I need the brain space to get on with finishing my waistcoat design to wow Meg tomorrow, and I am not going to let **BFF** stuff get in the way of my *Professional Attitude* and spoil all this for me when I have worked massively hard on it, so there!

(Except I think I might just have a *small* cry before I get started.)

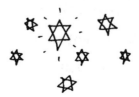

133

saturday morning,

our last day of filming (sniff!).

Well, I have woken up feeling 6 different ways at once this morning.

Firstly is *tired*: Last night I stayed up till 11.24 o'clock making my *Special Mission* waistcoat. The buttons I chose look really good, and I even finished off the little pocket bits on my own after Meg pointed me in the right direction. Now it looks like this

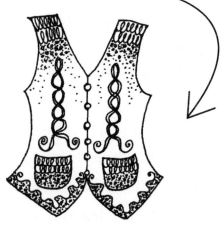

Secondly is *nervous*: This is with anticipativeness about what Meg'll think of the *Special Mission* waistcoat and whether she'll let an extra wear it in the actual film. I'm trying not to get too excited, 'cos I know it's not that likely, but...

Thirdly is actually *excited,* although, like I said, I am trying not to be it.

I never know whether to put in the "u"??

Fourthly is *worried*: This is 'cos of me and Jules falling out. I'm starting to wonder if this time it is the real end of our **BFF**ness.

Fifthly is upsetness because of *Fourthly.*

Sixethly (Sixtherly? Sixcethly?) is sadness 'cos it's the last day of filming. We are doing the wedding scene at a church in this village just outside town, both interiors and exteriors (see, I am only just learning film language when the experience is being cruelly snatched away from me!) and then that is **IT**, apart from the party, which I am going to now the knickershowing cringitis has worn off a bit. But even that won't be much fun if Jules hates me. Wearing a glammy film-star outfit does not make up for losing a **BFF** forever and ever.

But even when you are busy feeling six different things at once, time still keeps ticking away, so now I have to go, *byeeeeee*.

Date: Saturday the 16th of April.

Time: 9-ish o'clock.

Location: In Costume Van 1.

Total doughnuts scoffed: 3
(I'm nervous about
my waistcoat, OKAY?)

Oh wow, there is so much to tell you. I just
now got my bag from the extras' bus so I can
write straight in this journal again, and while I was
getting it I ran into Jules and Tilda. I smiled, and
Tilda smiled back, but then she quickly stopped
smiling when she saw Jules glaring at her. Jules
didn't smile at me, but instead she did that "*huh*"
sound again and walked right by with her nose
in the air. But even though that made me feel
completely sick with the unfairness, I have to stop
thinking about it now 'cos I can see Meg coming.
Time to show her my waistcoat! I just hope it's
good enough!

Date: Same.

Time: 22 past 10.

Location: On the steps of Costume Van 1.

Total doughnuts scoffed: Still only 3, have been too busy having amazing things happening to me to scoff any more!

Meg loved my waistcoat!

And someone is wearing it in the actual film.

And (prepare to faint!!!) it is being worn, not by an extra, but by *Daniel Blake* his actual self!!!

What happened was, Meg said she had a surprise for me, and she gathered up loads of stuff and told me to bring my waistcoat, and we went over to the trailers. That's where the stars hang out and we're not allowed round there normally (well, Meg is, obviously, but not me!). Meg knocked, and Daniel Blake called "Come in," and then there I was standing right in front of him! We had to fit all his clothes for the wedding scene, (meaning, yes, I got to see him in just his pants – *hee hee*!!!).

When he put on MY waistcoat I was in GOBSMACKED FLABBERGASTATION!!! Meg told me to do up the buttons for him, and so I have actually touched *Daniel Blake*! Can you believe it?!! I will never wash my hands again!!!

When the waistcoat was done up, Meg said, "You know, Daniel, Lucy designed and made that all by herself." Daniel looked at me like he'd only just noticed I was there, and I froze completely still in the middle of doing up the last button.

Then he smiled dazzlingly at me and said, "Is that true?" and I managed to do a tiny nod. He swivelled round to the full-length mirror and did this kind of looking-himself-up-and-down-and-admiring-the-waistcoat thing, and went, "This really is excellent. You're very talented. And you must be only, what—"

"Very nearly thirteen," I said quickly, before he

could come out with, like, *ten and a half* or something and spoil the moment.

"You should become a designer," he said. "I love designers, they're such creative people and true individuals."

"That's what I want to be," I blurted out, and then I started burbling away about winning the Fantasy Fashion Comp in my *Hey Girls!* magazine and styling a boy band. And all the time, another bit of my brain was thinking *Daniel Blake is noticing me in a good way!!!! Yessity-yes-yes!!!!*

Then Meg nudged me, and I realized I should stop gabbling. When I did I suddenly got struck with a **REVELATION** of how I really wished Jules was there to share the Daniel-Blake-meeting moment with me. I wanted *that* more than just meeting him on my own, and that's when I realized that me and Jules both think the other one has been unfair, so if one of us doesn't swallow our pride and say sorry then no one ever will and we will lose our **BFF**ness forever and ever.

Just then I spotted a picture of Daniel on the table, along with some papers. It was one of those glossy publicity-type ones that are called headshots. I quickly said, "Daniel, could you sign that picture for me, please?"

Daniel did the dazzling smile again and said, "Sure thing," and he was just about to write on it when I said, "Please could you make it out to my friend Jules, and could you put love instead of just best wishes and also do a few kisses?" Hopefully that will totally prove to her how much I want to be **BFF** again.

Daniel laughed and said, "Sure, seeing as it's for you," and scribbled away. Then he handed me the photo and even though his hand brushed mine and made me shiver I managed to remember my manners and go, "Thanks very much."

Then Meg said, "We'd better get going, Daniel. You know what Cat's like if things run late…"

Daniel rolled his beautiful green eyes and said, "Don't I just. What a nightmare, as you Brits say."

I realized they were talking about Caterina di Fablio and before I could stop myself I blurted out, "But I thought you were a couple. I read it in *Celeb* magazine."

Daniel laughed, going, "Don't believe everything you read! I just have to make nice so she doesn't throw a crazy while we're working, but she drives me nuts with all that Hollywood stuff. I like to keep it real, man. I go for real girls from the real world. You know, like designers!" he added with a wink.

So then I was over the actual moon with blissfulness, 'cos I am going to be a designer so he *would* actually fancy me except I'm too young. Well, not for long! I just have to wait a few years and then I can write him a letter and see if he remembers me, and if he does he might ask me out on my Fantasy Date!!! I was just thinking all that when Meg said, "Right, on that note we *really* should be going!" and bundled me out of the door, because I was in such complete joy I couldn't remember how to work my arms and legs.

And that was the end of my amazing meeting-Daniel-Blake experience.

I just hope the photo will be enough to convince Jules that I am making the first move of sorryness! (I think it would be best not to mention to her that Daniel nearly said he'll take my future self on a date, though!)

Oh, gotta go, Meg has just got back from Caterina di Fablio's dressing room, and it looks like she could do with a cup of tea!

Under the hairdryer
(how cool!)

I've just been in Hair and Make-up getting pampered, and now I'm under one of those big hairdryer things that goes over your whole head and looks like a brain-snatcher. The reason is because after I came back from the catering van with a cup of tea for Meg (and another doughnut for me), she looked at her watch and went, "Lucy, it's time for you to head off to Make-up."

I was just thinking, *Eh?* when she added, "And then come back in here for your costume fitting."

Then I was thinking, *Double eh?* and Meg looked across and saw my confusedness and said, "Didn't you see the schedule this morning?"

I went, "But I don't need to check it 'cos I'm not in the film."

Meg looked amazed, going, "But you are now, because you filled in for Jules during the gate scene!"

"Don't remind me," I said, thinking how that was the thing that wrecked me and Jules's **BFF**ness, maybe for good.

Then Meg said, "Well, you're in the wedding scene, of course. The whole cast has to be there. You'll be sitting in a pew with your friend Jules – Patrick's cooled down a bit about her now – so that'll be lovely, won't it?"

Right now I really don't know if it will be lovely or an utter disaster. I am really hoping the photo will be enough for Jules to forgive me.

Oh, I'm done apparently. *Byeeeeee!*

At home,
before the party.

Well, the stuff with Jules was a bit *hairy* and also *touch and go*.

First of all when we were on set she didn't want to link arms with me down the aisle and she kept trying to wriggle away. I had to use all my strength to hold on tight 'cos of the *Professional Attitude* thing of not making a fuss. I wanted to give her the photo and explain how I was sorry, but we weren't supposed to be talking. Daniel Blake came out at the last minute, and as he went past, he said, "Great waistcoat, Lucy," to me and winked.

I smiled back in happiness and then I looked at Jules's face, which was at maximum level on the *Dark and Stormy* scale.

"I can't believe it!" she hissed. "You met Daniel Blake and you—"

I stopped caring about the not talking thing then, because I knew that our friendship was on the *Brink of Dire Peril*. I whipped the signed photo out from my *Non-Heaving Bosom* (which was the only place I could keep it once the dress was on). I just held it out in front of me with my eyes closed, waiting for Jules to keep shouting at me. But instead she just gave me a massively rib-crunching hug and went, "You are such a fab **BFF**! You were right there with him and you thought about me! Sorry about blaming you for taking my scene when you were only trying to help."

And I went, "Sorry Patrick Moran wouldn't listen to you that the gate thing was really an accident."

And Jules went, "Sorry for getting *rivalrous* about a boy."

And I went, "Me too!"

And then Patrick Moran himself yelled, "Let's get on with the scene, girls, shall we, if that's okay with you!?" I somehow guessed he was being sarky

147

and not actually asking us nicely. Sadly he didn't get that me and Jules being **BFF** again is way more important than making a film!

So we did the scene 3 times, and we both had a completely *Professional Attitude*, i.e. we **DID NOT** leap on Daniel as he walked up the aisle, and we **DID NOT** stare at Daniel's bum during the actual weddingy bit, and we **DID NOT** shove Caterina di Fablio aside during the "You are now man and wife" bit and try to marry him instead. That shows we are totally cured of him, well, nearly, at least!

There was no "You may kiss the bride" bit 'cos apparently (according to Miss Brainbox Van der Zwan) that would be way too racy for Victorian times, even just with closed mouths and no tongues.

When me and Jules came off set we had another big squealy hug with Tilda, until Jules remembered the photo and thought she might be crushing it and had to rescue it from her *Heaving*

Bosom and flatten it out again.

Well, next, a **REVOLTING** thing happened. Seriously, don't read this bit while you're eating or it might put you off your food. The final scene we had to do was outside the church and then it would be a wrap (as in the end of filming, not as in a Chicken Mexicana sandwich type thing). Well, it was a wrap for us anyway, but not for the crew who are now heading off somewhere else without us (sob sob!).

We all came out of the church in a procession and then this horrible thing happened. Simon Driscott – oh, no I can hardly bear to tell you this –

Okay, I really can't stand to tell you this, so I will draw it as a cartoon.

Can you believe that?! Unluckily for me, Mr. Wildhair is leaving that bit in, because… "That's brilliant improvisation!" he yelled at Simon. "A peasant boy steals a kiss from a member of the country gentry as the procession goes by to show that he has been emboldened by John and Mariah's love conquering social barriers!"

I was glaring at Simon, and he went red and mumbled, "That's exactly why I did it. 'Twas the Muse! She inspired me!"

Well, all I can say is, when I find out who this Muse girl is, she is in **BIG** trouble!

Tilda came up, and I went, "Urgh! I cannot believe they are leaving that bit in!" and she went, "I know! They're sacrificing social reality for a ridiculous romantic ideal! I mean, as if one highly unlikely love story would cause the whole British class system to re-form at its very core! Dream on, Hollywood! In fact, there's no wedding at all at the end of the book, but instead Mariah has to marry a creaky old nobleman and *John the Honest*

Farmer's Son is discovered at the bottom of the Warwick family lake with a brick tied round his ankles."

I said, "I meant I cannot believe it for the reason of me getting kissed by the Prince of Pillockdom," which I have decided he definitely is again after that!

I will only say one more word about it, which is *shudder*.

Right, have to pull myself together and get ready for the party tonight!

10.17 o'clock,
after the party.

Mum thinks I'm asleep, but I am in actual fact writing this using the light-blocking towel trick. Hopefully she will never catch on about that otherwise my future journals will be very short and my design projects will never get finished. I'm really tired now, but my head is buzzing with everything that happened at the party and I'm far too excited to sleep.

Tonight was _soooooo_ amazing for lots of reasons. First of all, Dad came over before the party to pick us up, because if you were under 18 your parents got invited too. Alex was also coming 'cos of not being able to stay at home by himself.

Dad walked in the door, and the first thing he said was, "Sue, you are going to get changed and wash your hair before we go, aren't you?"

Mum gave him a _Look of Poison_ and said,

"Of course I am! Just give me half an hour. You may put the kettle on, but touch my éclairs and you're a dead man."

Then she swanned out and I swanned out after her. Alex went downstairs and played Connect Four with Dad while I changed into my glammy party outfit that I've put together.

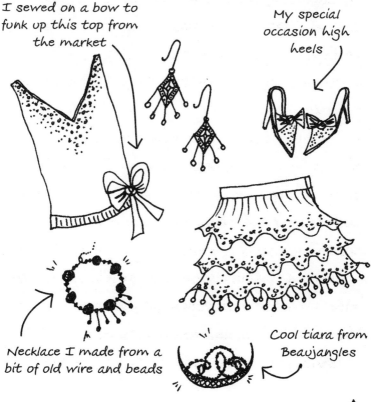

I sewed on a bow to funk up this top from the market

My special occasion high heels

Necklace I made from a bit of old wire and beads

Cool tiara from Beaujangles

Then I went downstairs again, and when Mum
came down, she looked like this

I am putting the before picture in to
show you the difference

Dad was so **ASTOUNDED** he didn't even say
anything.

Then it was time to go, and we all went out to
our car. Dad went to get in the passenger side and
Mum said, "Hang on, where do you think you're
going?"

Dad went, "But you never seem to mind not drinking."

And Mum said, "It's not that I don't mind, I just never have much choice. This is the first night out I've had for a month, so you can just be a Gentleman and drive me there and drink orange juice and then drive me home again."

Me and Alex had to clamp our hands on our mouths to stop ourselves from laughing, and Dad himself was too GOBSMACKED and FLABBERGASTED to say anything.

Then Mum made Dad hold the passenger door open for her. "Madam," he said, all sarkily, doing a low bow as she got in.

"About blooming time," she muttered, and I had a feeling she didn't just mean this evening. I had a feeling that she meant Dad should have been acting like a Gentleman for several years.

Anyway, it was *soooooo* cool walking into the Eagle Hotel where the party was and feeling like a proper film star. (I've never been in there before and it's totally glammy!) As we imagined, Daniel Blake was not there, but I didn't mind — well, not that much anyway. Then I suddenly spotted Jules, who was in a wild gothy outfit, like this

Dad was busy getting Mum a glass of wine and taking her coat to the cloakroom (on her orders!). "Poor Dad!" I went, and she said, "Don't give me *Poor Dad*! I'm doing him a favour, teaching him how to be a *Gentleman*!"

I said, "I thought those only existed in Victorian times, and now they are only the men's toilets."

Mum sighed. "No, Lu, they *are* still out there. I should have insisted on some *Gentlemanly Behaviour* from your father years ago, but I wasn't always this confident in myself. I'm really learning what I'm capable of."

I said, "Well, I think you're doing brilliantly," 'cos she really is, and we had a hug right there in the party.

Then Tilda arrived, and she'd made up a really cool hippy chick outfit all by herself (my style influence is obviously rubbing off on her), and also she was wearing make-up!

Then Meg came up and we all had a chat together, which was mainly about how fab

I was at being her assistant, which was completely embarrassing, but secretly I was also really pleased. Plus, Dad managed to only stare at Meg a tiny bit, so maybe the *Gentleman Training* is working after all.

Simon Driscott came up as well, and when we got asked to take our seats, he said, "Take them where?" He is *soooooo* not funny.

We watched the *rushes* (which is what you call the unedited scenes that were filmed over the past few days) on a big projector screen that came magically down from the ceiling. There were some great Jules bits, so she was really happy, and she didn't go one bit scowly when the gate scene came on with me in it instead of her. Tilda was brill in the milkmaid bits, and it was so *fantablious* watching Daniel Blake go up the aisle in **MY WAISTCOAT**. At that point Dad started clapping, and then Meg did too, and soon everyone was, although they probably didn't all know it was for me exactly.

Then it got to the Swain 2 stealing a kiss bit, so unluckily my actual parents got to watch me getting kissed by a boy (*urgh* – embarrassing or what?).

I had decided to start calling Simon the Prince of Pillockdom again for that, but because of my growing matureness I leaned over and whispered to him, "That was actually quite good."

Simon went all red and was going *splutter splutter* when I realized he thought I meant he was good at *kissing*, so I quickly added, "I mean you're good at *acting*, 'cos it looks like you're madly in love with me when in fact we are just sort of friends with no fancying going on whatsoever."

Simon stared at me for a second, then he went, "Excuse me, I just have to go and do something."

He slid along the row and went out, but I spotted him pretend-banging his head on the wall round the corner. *Huh* – boys are weird.

Then we had some more drinks and chatting, which is what adults do at parties instead of moshing and playing Spin the Bottle. We also had these cool little things called canapés that were like miniature meals you eat in one bite, like:

Asparagus wrapped
in this stuff like
wafer-thin ham
but redder

Diet curry!

No idea what
this was, but
very yummy!

Me and Jules and Tilda were trying them all, and Jules suddenly said, "I'm glad Daniel Blake isn't here, you know. It's much nicer to have a night out with my **BFF** without boys getting in the way."

Tilda beamed and said, "Absolutely, I couldn't agree more," before helping herself to this pastry thing with one prawn and a tiny sliver of red pepper balanced on top.

"Me too," I said, and I truly meant it. "Boys may come and go, but BFF are forever!"

And we all had a group hug of happiness then, which created a bit of a flaky-pastry-and-*crème-fraiche*-mess, but we didn't mind 'cos we were back together as a three with no silly *rivalrousness* between us, well, apart from over who got the last little salmon-balanced-on-a-pancake thingie (Jules did, BTW).

Tilda had to go then, and Mum decided we should too, even though it was still quite early, because (as she told Dad): "The children need to be in bed." I'm sure if she wasn't on her third glass of wine she would have remembered she really only meant Alex, because the very-nearly-teenager (i.e. me!) can go to bed way later than 9.30 p.m.

So I went to find Meg and say goodbye. I didn't know whether I should hug her or not, because although she has become sort of like my friend, she's still an adult. So first we did shaking hands (my idea), and then Meg started the kissing on both cheeks thing, which is so cool I wish I'd thought of it myself instead of the handshaking. Meg said, "I love your outfit, Lucy. Maybe you can wear it to the film premiere in London. You're invited of course, as Wardrobe Assistant."

That was so beyond cool I still didn't know what to say. Meg reckons it will be in about a year or something, 'cos it takes ages between making a film and it actually coming out, but she is definitely putting me down on the list!!!

So then

Whoops, Mum just burst in! She spotted the light under my door and I have been told to go to sleep this actual second or no more glammy parties till I'm 18! **DEFINITELY** don't want that to happen, so *byeeeeee*!!

<u>Sunday morning,</u>
still in my pyjamas with all
my stuff spread out on the
bed, eating toast and jam
(absolutely the ONLY way
to do homework!!!).

Tomorrow is school again and we have to take our Memory Boxes in to English. I am just finishing mine off this morning and here's what I'm putting in it:

1. Sugar sprinkles and jam smears. (I did have an actual doughnut, but you can guess where it went! I worked out I ate 17 doughnuts in one week – urgh!)

2. Fabric offcut to show the material I made Daniel's waistcoat out of.

3. One of the scarves from my
   re-designed costume.
   It's a good
   memory because if I'd
   never been creative enough to
   change my costume I wouldn't have ended
   up helping Meg, or dressing Daniel, or
   getting a corsety dress with an almost
   Heaving Bosom.

4. Picture drawn by me of
   Daniel's autograph as
   there is no way Jules will
   give me the real thing to
   shut away in a Memory
   Box. Instead she's getting a
   huge gothic-y black carved frame for it
   and putting it on the wall in her room.

5. Black tape from the church
   floor to show our marks.

6. Flower from Caterina di Fablio's wedding bouquet that I pressed under two of Tilda's heavy books.

7. A rubber glove like the one Tilda practised milking the cow on.

8. I couldn't think of how to show waiting to be called on set, so I have drawn an empty space, like this

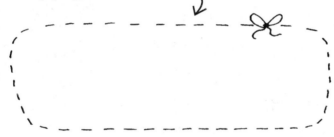

I wish I could put in the Memory Box about what an amazing experience it was to be in a film, even just as a billowy white sheet in the background, and especially as a proper character with a cool corsety dress. But I will just have to

keep those things in my own personal Memory Box (i.e. my brain!).

One thing that's not going in there is this note Meg gave me last night, 'cos I'm keeping it safely in my journal.

Megan McCarven
Hope Cottage, Little Snelling, Oxfordshire

Dear Lucy,

Thank you very much for all your help with the costumes on Passionate Indiscretions. Keep learning and experimenting and never let go of your dream to be a fashion designer! I'm sure that with your talent and dedication you will be very successful one day. Daniel Blake thinks so, after all!

If you ever want to come and help me again, you're always welcome. Also, it would be great if you wanted to keep in touch and tell me how your designs are going and about your ideas for future projects – because I think you'll have lots!

Love, Meg xxx

How totally cool is that?!!!

Well, I have to stop now 'cos me and Jules and Tilda are going to see the Daniel Blake movie that's on right now in town and dream about when it is actually *us* on the screen!!! Also, there is the more practical reason that I have run out of pages. I'll buy a new journal from the Spend and Save and write again soon…promise!

So this is me, signing off with my lovely new swirly signature I am inventing.

𝓑𝔂𝓮𝓮𝓮𝓮𝓮𝓮 for now!

Love,

Lucy Jessica Hartley

Lucy Jessica Hartley's Quiz

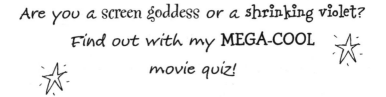

Are you a screen goddess or a shrinking violet?
Find out with my MEGA-COOL
movie quiz!

1) You're asked to read out a poem in assembly. How do you react?

A) In public? You'd rather change your name and move to Bulgaria!

B) You're really pleased — but you'll spend the whole week practising to make sure it goes smoothly.

C) A poem? You ditch that idea and offer them your two-hour one-woman show instead.

2) Which of these pictures best represents you?

A)   B)   C)

3) You spot a gorge film star in your local shopping mall. Do you:

A) Pretend to have some urgent staring at the ground to do while going bright red.

B) Rummage for a pen, take a deep breath, and ask for his autograph.

C) Strike a pose and wait for him to come and ask for **YOUR** autograph!

Mostly As: Oh dear, you need a confidence boost! Stop trying to blend into the background and start acting like a star instead — you'll soon feel like one!

Mostly Bs: You love supporting others, but when your own chance comes, you take it! Well done — you're a perfect mix of demure and diva!

Mostly Cs: You love the limelight and you've certainly got star quality — but be sure to give your friends a chance to shine too!

Totally Secret Info about Kelly McKain

Lives: In a small flat in Chiswick, West London, with a fridge full of chocolate.

Life's ambition: To be a showgirl in Paris 100 years ago. *(Erm, not really possible that one! – Ed.)* Okay, then, to be a writer – so I am actually doing it – yay! And also, to go on a flying trapeze.

Star sign: Capricorn (we're meant to be practical).

Who would you most like to be stuck in a lift with: A lift-repair man (see star sign). Oh, and he'd have a full lift-fixing tool kit and a giant Toblerone.

Fave colour: Purple.

Fave animal: Monkey.

Ideal pet: A purple monkey.

Five seconds of fame: Being an extra on a TV show. The hardest thing is pretending to chat while making no noise at all! (Very difficult for me!)

Fave hobbies: Hanging out with my BFF and gorge boyf, watching *Friends*, going to yoga and dance classes, and playing my guitar as badly as Lucy's dad!

Don't miss more of Lucy's hilarious journals

Makeover Magic

Lucy Jessica Hartley is a style queen, so when a geeky new girl starts at school, she comes up with a fab Makeover Plan to help her fit in.

0 7460 6689 9   £4.99

Fantasy Fashion

Lucy's fave mag is running a competition to design a fantasy fashion outfit and Lucy is determined to win the fab prize - whatever it takes!

0 7460 6690 2   £4.99

Boy Band Blues

Lucy has been asked to style a boy band for a Battle of the Bands competition and she's mega-excited about it - it's just a shame she hates big-headed lead singer Wayne!

0 7460 6691 0   £4.99

Picture Perfect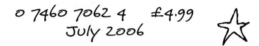

Lucy decides to throw a big surprise party for Tilda's 13th birthday – but will crossed wires wreck her efforts, and their friendship?

0 7460 7062 4   £4.99
July 2006

Style School

School fashion guru Lucy sets up a Style School in the loos, with lessons in accessories, hair and make-up. But what will happen when the School Uniform Police (aka Mr. Cain) finds out?

0 7460 7063 2   £4.99
October 2006

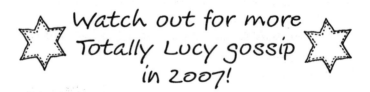

Watch out for more Totally Lucy gossip in 2007!

To Kevin and Jo, with love.

Thanks a gazillion to Gaelle Hobbs for all the wardrobe department info (especially the fake-vomit story – yum!!)

JFM MJJASOND/06
ISBN 0 7460 7061 6